WALKIN'
WITH THE
BEAST

DANNY VALDEZ

2013   SUN DOG PRESS   NORTHVILLE, MICHIGAN

Printed in the United States of America   First Edition

Dedicated to Billy Holliday Valdez. This is our history, son. If you know where you come from, it's a lot easier to know where you're going.

And to all my brothers and sisters out there doing it everyday in the call centers, minimum wage jobs, bus stops and public assistance offices—you gotta keep your head up.

Acknowledgments

Bullet-proof love is extended to—

My mother, for her unwavering support and understanding at my lowest moments.

My father, for trying to teach me the way and giving me a home when I had none.

My sister, for always having my back.

Matt W. Booze, Uriah Gable, and Donnie Mauldin,
for being the brothers I never had.

Bullet-proof unity is extended to—

Monty Owen, my partner in crime, Rock 'n' Roll compadre and best friend. Your friendship and wise words have always been a supreme inspiration. We are bound by Ka-tet and I wouldn't have it any other way.

Travis "T-Bird" Johnston, for being a friend when I had none and for being the funniest, most quick-witted motherfucker I've ever known.

Ian Davison, for setting my mind free, showing me the glory of Punk Rock, and for being the fifth member of the Valdez family.

Nick Feratu, for giving me my typewriter and the encouragement to hit these keys and tell these stories.

Bullet-proof appreciation is extended to—

Robbie Pfeffer of Tempe Starving Artist, for being my greatest local supporter/publisher and for being down when no one else was.

John Martin, Dan Fante, and Pamela Wood for their kind words and support of an unknown writer.

Last, but not least—

Al & Judy Berlinski of Sun Dog Press, for taking a chance on me, for their Samurai dedication to putting out the best book possible, for their unshakable belief in the words I write, for postponing their retirement to make this book, and for finally making my voice heard.

Under the driving inspiration of:

Charles Bukowski, Henry Rollins, Jeffrey Lee Pierce, Eddie Cochran, Walt Whitman, Nicolas Winding Refn, Louis C. K., Jim Morrison, Hank Williams, Sr., Dan Fante, Martin Scorsese, Sanyika Shakur, Tom Waits, Jim Jarmusch, Muddy Waters, Howlin' Wolf, and that boy from Tupelo, Elvis Aaron Presley.

TABLE OF CONTENTS

"In the still of the night, I walk with the Beast
in the heat of the night, I sleep with the Beast
who slipped so deep inside me
and rots the love right out of me

I prayed to Elvis on my knees
to take this thing from around me
or snap it with a thundercrack
and change my blues to black

but, how did my love surround me
with such a dead thing around me,

I'm just walkin' I'm just walkin'
I'm just walkin'
Walkin' with the Beast . . ."

—Jeffrey Lee Pierce

Part One

HOMELESS LITTLE BOYS

As a child
I had a fear that one could
become homeless
fairly easily.
I'd see a homeless man on the corner
and wonder how he got that way.
"Mom?"
"What Daniel?"
"What if I grow up to be homeless? Like that man on the corner."
"Mijo . . . I'd never let that happen, you'll always have a home."
She did put my mind at ease,
but at the same time
I wondered,
is that what the homeless man's mom
told him
when he was a little boy?

Sometimes the old man would take me with him on his round of favorite bars. When I was a little boy. He would always order me Shirley Temples with extra cherries, while he drank Budweiser and pounded down shot after shot between sips. He'd flirt with the female bartenders and make small talk with all the old barflies and crack them up with his jokes.

Everyone seemed to know his name.

He had nothing but friends in each bar we visited.

I loved these nights with Dad.

"You're pretty lucky to have a dad like Big Dan. He's a good guy," the lady bartenders would tell me.

The thing I loved most was sitting high on the bar stool and playing with the touch-screen game machine (especially movie trivia) while Dad bullshitted with everyone in the bar.

Sometimes we'd play pool, and the old man usually let me win. If he didn't let me win, though, he'd let me get REAL close, then, at the last minute, sink all the balls and laugh that loud guttural laugh of his. The kind that would make his belly shake up and down.

I'd get mad at him and ask, "Why didn't you let me win, Dad?"

"Because, son, you can't always be *given* a win. You have to earn it. We all lose from time to time. Hell, as you get older, you'll find that you lose more than you win. Get used to it."

"At pool?"

"At anything. Losing is a big part of life. I'm trying to teach you something here, boy."

I learned a lot from those days and nights at the bar with my old man.

The art of conversation.

How to talk to women. And how to treat them.

Respect for the elderly.

The old-timers that sat at the far end of the bar, staring into their drinks and tapping their thumbs on the glass . . . they wouldn't talk much, but they always came by to pat Dad on the back and thank him for the drink.

Oftentimes, the lady bartenders would let my old man get behind the bar. He'd serve himself and entertain anyone in his way. Wherever he moved, he made friends.

I looked up to him so much at that age. I wanted to grow up and be just like him—

the funniest guy in the room,

the ladies man,

the friend of the cranky old-timers,

the stand-up guy.

One night, on the drive home, I remember saying, "I wanna be just like you, Dad."

"No, son, you don't wanna be like me."

I could never understand his answer.

He seemed so great.

In my young eyes, the old man was full of magic.

THE WRONG BITCH TO FUCK WITH

My mom and I went out
driving around from bar to bar
a lot,
looking for my old man.
Usually we'd find him pretty early on.
And then, on the drive home, with my mom yelling at him,
my four-year-old ass sat in the back seat
having to listen to it all.

Those were the
good nights,
the easy & calm nights.

But this one night, I remember,
shit really got crazy.
My mom went inside his favorite bar
with me on her hip.
The bartender told her he had just left
with some blonde lady.
So we sat in the car, in the dark, and waited.
His Harley was parked out front,
so we knew he'd be back.
My mom chain-smoked
and sipped icy Mountain Dew
from her green metal thermos.
She had fire in her eyes,
gasoline in her veins.
My mom was really gonna let him have it
"and that blonde bitch, too," she said.

The bar was next door to a 7-11.
Two lowlife motherfuckers were
standing around.
They saw my mom and I sitting there.
One of them yelled at her,
"Watcha lookin' at bitch?"
"I ain't lookin' at you, shut the fuck up."
They didn't say anything,

just started walkin' away.
Out of nowhere, though,
the shit-talkin' lowlife was next to her window.
He reached in and grabbed my mom by the arm.
I was really scared, I remember.
"Watcha got to say now? Huh bitch?"
My mom reached for her pistol
with her free hand,
while the lowlife kept talking,
threatening to rape her in front of her son.
Within seconds, the black 9mm pistol
was unholstered and shoved into his nose.
His eyes were as wide as they got.
His hands now up in the air,
he was shaking & trembling.
My mom pulled back the hammer,
it made that terrifying click.
"I AM a bitch. The WRONG bitch to fuck with tonight."
"Be cool lady. Becoolladybecool. Don't shoot, don't shoot."
The gun was now pressed
into his sunburned, pockmarked cheek.
"Get the fuck away from my car."
And just like that, off he ran into the darkness.

I had fully expected her to
blow his head off, right there in front of me.
She asked if I was okay.
I nodded yes and she kissed my forehead.
She stood outside the car then,
next to Dad's Harley,
pacing back and forth,
her adrenaline really pumping now,
smoking and drinking soda
from that green metal thermos.

I don't know how much time passed,
but eventually a little red car pulled up.
My dad and the blonde got out.
When he saw my mom, he sighed and said,
"Ahhh fuck me."
The blonde tried to go into the bar,
but Mom blocked her entry saying,

"Uh . . . ah. What the fuck were you doing with MY man?"
The blonde looked to my dad for help.
"Danny?" she cried.
"Rhonda, nothing happened. I just got some blow from her.
That's all."
"Bullshit," she yelled.
The blonde again tried to go into the bar,
and again my mom stood in her way.
By now the blonde was pissed.
"Bitch, get the fuck outta my way."
"You fuckin' whore," my mom shrieked,
smashing the green metal thermos to her face.
Then she dropped it
and began throwing wild punches to the blonde's
face and head.
My dad let her get in a few good hits,
then pulled her off.
The blonde's face was
red, swollen, and bloodied.
She finally ran inside.

"Get in the truck," my mom ordered Dad.
"I'll take the Harley," he told her.
"Get in the damn truck," she repeated.
And he did, too afraid not to.
They argued all the way home.
The old man stuck to his story—
that it was just a drug deal.
She wasn't havin' it.
They told me to go to bed,
but I stayed up,
peeking around the corner,
watching them argue.
The old man was too drunk & coked out.
Finally she just threw a hard right
and layed him out on the kitchen floor.
I heard her call him an asshole
as I pulled my Batman blanket up to my chin.
Shit.
My mom was tougher than Batman.

How Can You Not Like Tabasco?

My father always tried to teach me Spanish, but, at five years old, I had no interest in learning Spanish words. He would say something, then ask me to repeat it, but I would just say, "Blahblahblah." After a while he'd get pissed and give up. But the one thing he did teach me, besides a few select curse words, was how to count to ten.

Our kindergarten class was learning how to count to ten in Spanish. Well, my teacher was white and one day, while counting along, she got to three.

"Tres." She said it like "trace."

I immediately interrupted her, "That's not how you say it."

"Excuse me?" she asked, surprised.

"It's tres, not trace. I'm Mexican, I know."

"Okay, well, Daniel, I'm the teacher—"

"But that's not how you say it, though."

"Daniel. I—am—the—teacher. You are the student—"

"You're just a *puta*."

"WHAT?!"

"A bitch," I translated to English.

She sent me home with a note, telling my parents what I'd said and giving me a "red light" for the day. Being a naive five-year-old, I walked in the door and handed the note to my mom. I don't know why I wasn't scared of what would happen to me, probably because I'd never really gotten into trouble at school before. My mom stood reading it, her eyes getting wider and more white in the way that terrified me. The scary thing was she didn't scream or yell. No. She just said, "You wait until your dad gets home."

I began to cry.

"You better dry it up!"

All afternoon I sat in my room like a man facing his execution, sitting in his cell, counting down the minutes. After sundown my father finally came home. My bedroom door swung open, and there he stood, reeking of sweat and smelling of the Arizona sun, his hardhat and work gloves still in his hands, .

"Get out here. NOW."

I hurriedly walked out to the kitchen. Slowly my dad began to speak.

"Spanking you won't work, taking away your toys or your Nintendo won't make you listen. But maybe this will," he said, pulling a bottle of red Tabasco sauce from the cupboard and setting it on the table.

I'd seen the old man put it on his eggs and just about everything else he ate besides his cereal. Just the smell of it across the table burned my nose.

"You think it's okay to talk to the teacher like that? Huh?!" my father said, kneeling down, his large brown hands gripping my shoulders, his bloodshot eyes piercing into mine.

"You are the student. She is the teacher. You think you know it all? You don't know shit. Is calling her a name, having respect for an adult?"

I stood silent, just staring at him.

He quickly swatted my stomach to get my attention, "Huh?"

"No."

"No, what?"

"No, that's not having respect."

"No, it's not," he said. "Rhonda, gimme the bottle."

"No, no, no, no!" I began to frantically cry, covering my mouth and trying to break his grip.

"Hey, this is what happens, son. For every choice you make, there is a consequence. You can't just do whatever you want. Nobody can. Not even me. Now here . . . take your medicine, son."

"It's medicine? I thought it was chili . . ."

My mother stood, her hand over her mouth, her stomach shaking with laughter. She finally turned away, still laughing.

"Take your medicine, son. It means, take your punishment. And take it like a man. You fucked up, so pay for it."

"Okay," I said with a sniffle. I watched my father unscrew the green cap.

"Stick out your tongue."

I did as I was told and felt the one little tiny drop hit my tongue. Steam might have come out my ears, I don't remember. But I ran through the house screaming and wailing like a goddamn banshee. I could hear my mom and dad, both laughing their asses off. I turned to see their faces—red, with tears flooding their eyes as they watched me struggle to climb the counter and get my mouth under the faucet.

Tears and drool poured down my face as I splashed water into my mouth. But it didn't help; it only seemed to make it worse. My tongue burned so much, I knew I could blow flames into the room.

"Danny . . ." my mother said in a *you poor thing* tone.

My dad, smiling, poured me a little glass of milk, which I downed until the burning finally ceased. Like a flame snuffed out, it just stopped. I remember trying to catch my breath, saying, "I can't . . . breath . . . I . . . can't . . . breath . . ."

Then my mom lifted me up into her arms and my father ran his big fingers through my hair and kissed my cheek.

They were just trying to teach me the law of cause and effect. Crime and punishment. And it worked, but in a way they might not have expected.

To this day, if I'm eating somewhere with friends and get a whiff of Tabasco in the air, I feel anger and fear and am reminded of that day.

And if someone asks, "What's the matter? You don't like Tabasco? How can you not like Tabasco?"

Ha! Well let me tell ya' about it, pal.

GET THE GUNS! HANDLE THIS!

I remember
my dad coming in through the front door,
blood-stained all down
the front of his shirt
from a big open cut
right between his eyes.
I ran to him and hugged onto his leg.
"What happened, Dad?"
He patted my head
and took off his leather jacket.
"Ahhh, I got into a fight, son."
"YOU DID!?"
"Yeah . . . some motherfucker busted a bottle on my face. See?"
he said, showing me the jagged cut. "You should see the other guy.
I busted him up real good."
"But then why are you bleeding?"
"'Cause it was my fault, I wasn't paying attention. Hit me when I
wasn't looking. See that's why I'm always telling you . . . be
aware of your surroundings . . . at all times. When you don't pay
attention, this is what happens."
"Let's get the guns, Dad . . . let's go handle this shit."
He walked down the hall
into the bathroom
to clean himself up
and lick his wounds,
all the while laughing that infamous, gut-shaking laugh of his.

I'll Clean My Room, Don't Shoot Me, Mom

Five years old
and I was cleaning my room.
Well,
I was supposed to be cleaning my room,
but my Ninja Turtles were fighting
the Footclan—
cleaning would just have to wait.
In the living room,
my parents were unloading a new shipment
of guns.
AK-47s from the Middle East.
My mom & dad
were pouring sand out of the guns
and into a bucket on the floor,
cleaning them all,
getting them ready
to be sold.
My mom was almost done
cleaning out one of the guns
when my father asked,
"Is Daniel cleaning his room?"
"He's supposed to be."
"Go check on him, babe."
"Yeah."
Cradling a gun in her arms,
not even thinking about it,
she opened my door
to find me laying on the floor,
Raphael & Leonardo fighting Shredder.
"Goddamnit, Daniel! Clean this room, now."
I saw the barrel of the gun in the doorway, pointing down.
"I'm sorry, Mom! Don't shoot! I'll clean my room! I'll clean it!"
"Good. Get it done," she said, holding back a smile,
trying her best to stay in stern mom mode.
The door slammed shut and I got up.
Standing in front of the pile
of toys and clothes,

I heard my father and my mother
laughing hilariously
from the living room.
My parents didn't have timeouts
or some bullshit parenting methods
to help motivate me.
No.
They had AK-47s.

CHILDREN CAN DIE AND BE ASSHOLES

I was six years old
when I found out that kids could die.

There was this one family at my grandma's church—
the only black family
in the entire congregation.
The mother
was petite, wore thick glasses, and played piano during church.
The father
was greatly obese, with thinning hair, and a permanent smile.
Their two boys
were four and twelve years old.

The night of their death
I saw them at church.
Service had just gotten out
and I was running wild with my two friends,
both a grade higher than me.
We ran across the large stage
and jumped into the huge bathtub
they used for baptisms.

The four-year-old boy,
only an hour away
from Death's grip,
said to me with a big, genuine smile,
"Hi Daniel."
But he was only four.
Practically a baby, I thought.
I was running with the big kids.
No time for babies.
So I turned back to running around with my friends,
ignoring his friendly greeting.

An hour later
that little boy's dad
pulled the family Lincoln Town Car over on the freeway.
Flat tire.

While the dad walked around the back of the car,
the wife and two boys waited inside.
Some fucking drunk
slammed into the car.
The dad watched the car
fly forward and burst into flames.
The smiling four-year-old
burned to death that night.
The twelve year old
suffered severe brain damage and died two days later.
And the father died of a heart attack a few months after that.
The mother's face, chest, back, neck, arms, and hands
bore charred and bubbling skin.
That piano-playing lady of the Lord
buried her whole family.

A decade later,
I sat there,
a teenager back at my grandma's church
for mother's Day.
The burned former mommy and wife
still sat and played that piano.
For some reason
she was still working for the big guy upstairs.

I couldn't understand it then, and I still don't:
I didn't say "Hi"
to that doomed little boy that night.
That was the first time I'd ever felt like an asshole.
That was when I was six years old.

The City Faggots In Cowboy Hats

It was hard to get used to.
Hard to take.
Not my parents being divorced,
that was actually better
for everybody.
No, I mean
my mom changing the way that she did.
At ten years old,
I didn't really understand it.
I couldn't yet.
My mother had gotten knocked up/married
at just eighteen years old
to a hard partying, longhaired biker.
After that, she spent her time with me
and my sister.
But when they got divorced,
everything changed,
just fucking *everything*.
She wasn't cooped up
with us kids all the time anymore.
No, she had friends, boyfriends,
they were all a part of that whole
urban cowboy scene.

When it all first started,
it wasn't so bad.
She'd go out on Friday or Saturday night,
be home by midnight or one o'clock,
and then she'd spend the rest of the weekend
with just us.
It was okay.
I was actually really happy for her.
So was my sister.
She seemed a lot happier,
smiled more than ever.

But then it turned into
two nights a week.
Then three.
And she started bringing the party home
after the bars closed
—an entire western entourage:
her friends Christy, Cassandra, and Big Kara,
along with three or four
random men.
"Cowboys"—
They'd come in the house like
a goddamn tornado
of denim and boots.
They'd blare music at 3 a.m.
Metallica's "Enter Sandman"
and Nine Inch Nails' "Closer."
I'd see my mom and her friends
bumping and grinding,
dancing dirty,
their tongues in the mouths
of these strangers,
these city faggots in cowboy hats and
yelling and slurring along with the song
"I WANNA FUCK YOU LIKE AN ANIMAL!"
And I'd beg,
plead with her,
"Mom, please, just turn the music down and stop. Please."
"Go to fuckin' sleep then, if you don't like it.
S' my fuckin house."
Then I'd go to my bedroom and wait,
and wait and wait
for the blasting speakers, the thumping bass
to stop.
But at least she was home.

I can't count how many other nights
I waited up for her—
past the dawn of the following day—
and she didn't come home,
didn't call me back
after paging her beeper

dozens of times.
Sitting there on the couch,
weeping for my mother
I assumed the worst—
that she was dead somewhere.
It happened too many times to count
and more than I care to remember.
One time
my Dad was in town
on a break between jobs
on the road.
He agreed to baby sit my sister and I
while Mom went out.
"I'll be back by one," she had said.
But she didn't come back until
late the next morning.
I awoke to my dad yelling at her for
the rug burns on her knees.
I didn't understand what that meant,
like I said, I was just ten years old.
But I had an idea.
I knew it had something to do with sex . . .

I was more aware than either of them thought,
and I remember everything.
Like what came next.
The seemingly endless parade of boyfriends.
Some of the guys would try and
buy me off with gifts,
but I wanted no part of it.
When my parents split up,
my Father told me that I was
the man of the house.
I took it pretty seriously.
I was very territorial
for such a skinny little kid
with buck teeth and spiky hair.
One time this urban cowboy
(a John Travolta wannabe motherfucker)
came over to the house.
My sister and I were playing in the backyard

and this prick thought it'd be funny to
take my Super-Soaker squirt gun
and hose me down with it.
At first it was fun.
Most of the guys she brought around
just ignored me,
but then he took the shit too far.
Wouldn't stop soaking me
in the face,
right in my eyes.
But I knew how to put a stop to it.
Real fucking quick.
I went inside the house
and picked up his nice Stetson cowboy hat.
When I returned outside,
he was still standing there
with my Super-Soaker still in his hand
and that wise-ass smirk on his face.
That is until he saw that black hat in my little hand.
Then his face got serious and real mean
as I held the Stetson over a mud puddle.
Now I was the one smiling
as I said,
"Now are you gonna give me my gun?
Or do I have to ruin this nice hat?"
He looked to my mother
"Well, what's it gonna be, cowboy?"
"Daniel!" my mother shouted.
He handed the gun back
and that was the last I ever saw of him.

After nearly two years of this endless cycle
of booze and partying and
dancing to Metallica at three in the morning
and the endless barrage of urban cowboys
it finally,
mercifully ended.
She met a real cowboy—
a rodeo rider and toughman fighter—
a decent man
that wasn't like the others

20

and treated us fairly.
And they got married
and everything that happened—
all that shit—
was just a memory.
She never really talked about it,
but I never let her forget
all the nights spent crying and waiting for her
to come home safe.

First, she had always been there for me,
never left my side;
but she changed and then she was out all night
and the old man was on the road.
I was all alone.
It felt like

a nightmare

just trying to keep it all together.
But it passed,
like all things eventually do,
one way
or another.

It was another night of babysitters, late-night television, and waiting up for Mom. Just after midnight, the doorbell rang. The babysitter answered the door and it swung open to reveal my dad . . . with his 19-year-old girlfriend.

"Dad!" my sister and I both shouted, running into his big, brown arms.

"I thought you were in Buffalo?" I asked, hugging him tight.

"Yeah, I was. I'm just in town for tonight, though. You and your sister get dressed. We're going to the store."

"Uhhh . . . Rhonda didn't say anything about you picking them up," the babysitter said.

"It's fine. I got them now. Here." He handed her a hundred dollar bill. "You can go."

"Whatever," she said, gathering up her purse and shit.

We walked into Walmart, my dad's girlfriend pushing a shopping cart.

"What are we doing here, Dad?" I asked.

"You and your sister can get anything you want."

"Anything?"

"Yeah, son, any ONE thing."

We were so excited. Not just about the toys, but to have the old man back, even just for one night, was the greatest gift. He'd been on the road, working for nearly six months now, and we both missed him terribly. Moving down the rows of the toy aisles, passing all the Spiderman and X-Men toys, I found what I wanted. It was a video game that you strapped to your head, the screen was clear plastic with a lite-up, red LED screen. A Batman video game, a cheap little thing, but it was what I wanted. My sister got a bike.

We got back to the house and my mom was there with two of her girlfriends. My dad said he had to go, but that he'd be back in a few months. Back for good. He kissed us goodbye and went outside. Mom followed him out. I could hear her yelling at him about how he needed to pay his fucking child support. More cursing back and forth, then a car door slammed, the engine started up, and the car drove away. My mom came back inside.

"Get your jackets on, we're leaving."

We drove a long time in the night. I had on sunglasses my dad had given me. I was crying and I didn't want anyone to see. We finally got to a house in the middle of the desert, and got out of the car. One of my mom's friends put her hands on my shoulder.

"Aw, honey, you don't have to wear those sunglasses. No one is gonna see you cry."

". . . fuck off . . ."

"What?"

"Nothing."

And inside, it went like it usually did—my mom and her girlfriends dirty dancing, bumping, and grinding with their urban cowboys, to Metallica's *The Black Album*. My sister was asleep on the couch, while I played my cool new video game. One of my mom's friends grabbed my arm and pulled at me.

"Come on! Dance with us!" she slurred, wasted and stinking of tequila.

"Leave me the fuck alone, goddamnit!"

"Gawd! This boy's got a dirty mouth over here! He cusses like an adult."

"Daniel! Quit being a little shit!" my mom shouted, before the cowboy pushed his tongue into her mouth.

Eventually it ended. They paired up with the cowboys and went to their back rooms. At last, silence. Just me and Batman . . . lit up in a red light. The sun was just beginning to rise. I could hear moans and slapping noises from down the hall. I took off the video game headset and pulled the blanket up over my head, wondering just when the fuck my dad would come back into town and all this shit would be over.

LOST LOFT

Mrs. Wong was a real progressive lady.
I didn't know it at the time,
but now that I think about it,
she was a total hippie.
She once built a wooden loft in the classroom.
Two levels with a ladder.
I fucking loved that loft.
The whole class helped set it up.
The wood was soft and nearly naturally white.
When it was finally done,
we had a read-a-thon.
(We sat around the room with blankets and snack foods and read
for hours.)
Being one of the lucky few, I got to sit
and read, eating my lunchable
in the high upper level of the loft . . .
letting the books take me somewhere else entirely.
I loved Mrs. Wong for the loft.
She was one of the good ones, the rare ones.

Then "The Man" took it all away.
Some higher up said it violated
fire code.
They took it apart like thieves in the night.
One morning we came in and it was gone.
We read books on the carpet,
or at our desks after that.

The first of many lost battles.
Ahhh.

No, It's Not Cool

By the time second grade rolled around, the school came up with some new thing—a "multi-graded" classroom. First, second, and third grade all in one room.

My teacher was Mrs. Wong, a middle-aged Latina, married to a Chinese man. They had four or five kids.

The class was all seated on the floor while she told us a story about how bad Communism had been for her husband's family in China.

"It got so bad that my husband's brother tried to swim from China to Japan. On his way, he was attacked by sharks. They ate both his legs right off, just tore them to ribbons. He would've died there if a fishing boat hadn't picked him up."

"Cool!" I said, excitedly. I had been reading about sharks and shark attacks.

Mrs. Wong stopped and looked at me with that face that she had that told us *"oh-oh."* The entire class turned and stared at me.

"No, Daniel . . . it's not cool. He barely survived and he has nightmares about it all the time."

I pictured a legless Chinese man, tossing and turning in his bed, screaming out into the night.

". . . that was inappropriate. Now is there anything that you'd like to say?"

"I'm sorry, Mrs.Wong," I said, my head down.

I could feel the hard stares from my classmates.

"Thank you. Now, have any of you . . ."

Mrs. Wong was a good teacher and a real nice lady. I was the insensitive asshole that was

really, really, really into sharks.

Not About to See Your Light

Whenever I would ask too many questions or asked the wrong kind of questions a woman would take me out of the Sunday School classroom, walk me down the hall through the double doors and into the big church where all the adults were. Squeezing my hand like a vice, *her* walking too fast and *me* just moving my little legs to keep up. She'd find my grandparents (my parents only went to church on holidays), turn me over to them, and then I'd have to sit in boring-ass-big-church.

My grandmother made sure I was actively involved in church and indoctrinated with her beliefs from the time I was born. She was an Evangelist Pentecostal, the most extreme form of Christianity: speaking in tongues, prophecy, spiritual "gifts," all that stuff. She picked me up twice a week—Sundays and Wednesdays—from the ages of four to ten. I was in something similar to the Boy Scouts called "Royal Rangers." We did typical scout type stuff like camping, knot tying, fire starting, survival techniques. What I remember most, though, was this little fake campfire they made for us in our classroom within the church. It was six logs crisscrossed, with one of those light bulbs that came to a pointed tip, unevenly painted in red, yellow, and orange. We'd sit around that thing during prayer request time. That was the time we made our wishes to God and told him what we wanted or needed him to do. Us "troubled" kids—we prayed for our parents. Us kids whose parents didn't come to church—everything they said that was a sin, our parents did: Drink, smoke, curse, gamble, look at naked lady magazines or videos, not go to church. All those were sins our parents did. They had us all terrified that our parents were going to burn in hell unless we could "save" them. They advised us to try and minister to our parents, get them to come to church and change their wicked ways. That's a lot to weigh on little kids. A kid in my class, one of my friends, he leaned over during a lesson and whispered in my ear, "I don't wanna be an orphan in heaven; I'd rather be in hell with my family." But to me that was nothing.

26

What really scared me, kept me on constant edge, was the rapture. When angels' trumpets would sound in the air, those "right" with God would be taken up into the sky, to heaven. They said even those in graveyards would come out of the grave and into the sky. The world would then be given over to Satan who would kill all Christians and make everyone get the mark of the beast.

They showed us videos by some guy named Carmen and they talked about it incessantly. They spoke of guillotines chopping off the heads of Christian martyrs—those that refused to take the number of the beast, 666. They said the only way to get into heaven if you were "left behind" after the rapture had taken place was to give your life up for God; that got you a one-way ticket to heaven.

Our Sunday school teachers and later our youth pastors described the most horrific things to us. They said you wouldn't be able to buy food, have a job, a house, nothing without getting the mark of the beast, which, of course, would send your soul straight to hell when you died. I became a paranoid, nervous wreck. Constantly scared that the rapture would happen like when I was at school perhaps. (They said it could happen at ANYtime.) And it would be chaos on the streets; I'd never be able to find my family, if that happened. I worried myself sick over it throughout the day, like clockwork, asking God to forgive me of any sins I may have committed, just in case the rapture did happen. So I could get into heaven.

At nine years old I went to my first Christian summer camp for a week, up in the woods of northern Arizona. I would end up going many times after that. The first year our camp counselor had this whole collection of Maglite flashlights all held in a fancy leather carrying case. He'd pull one out, then start shining the light on us—us boys in our underwear—then hit a few of us in the butt with those flashlights. The guy didn't hit me, but he hit my friend, a poor & tough kid that came from the ghettos of Mesa. This kid didn't take no shit. He called the guy a motherfucker and slugged him in the side of his fat face.

The big adult grabbed him by the back of his head and screamed at him, "I'm gonna call your parents! You are outta here! What's your father going to say?"

"Fuck you, bitch! I don't even have a dad!"

The man grew silent for only a few seconds, before coming back with, "Well, your mother is---"

"Hey! But you hit him first!" one of the other boys yelled.

"Yeah, with the flashlight!" I chimed in.

The counselor chilled out after that and tried to apologize to my friend, but he just turned on his side away from him, softly crying to himself.

Some years later as a young teenager in Oregon I went to another summer camp. Going in there most everybody, all the guys in my cabin, none of us gave a shit. All any of us had on our minds was the girls at the camp. Sitting through sermons about abstinence, snickering to ourselves, whispering to each other "Fuck that. I'm losing my virginity the first chance I get." We all agreed.

But by the second night things took a strange and serious turn. The counselors started in about the rapture, the apocalypse, the end. For nearly two hours at a time they went on and on. They all knew exactly what they were doing. It was basic psychology. They were scaring the fuck out of us, citing bullshit as facts about certain prophecies that have come true, taking scripture and bending it to meet real world events. Mentally breaking us down, minute by minute. All my buddies that acted like they could care less, were now crying and sobbing, their hands in the air, going right along. Hell, I was too. Some started speaking what sounded like gibberish, repeating certain vocal patterns, but without actual words. Gibberish. The pastors called it their "prayer language."

The preacher screamed, "Oh, she's speaking to the Lord, folks! That's right!"

He pointed to a girl screaming at the top of her lungs "Shiiii da da da d shiiiii do do do!" We watched her entire body shake as tears poured from her face.

Our youth pastor had a little vial of oil around his neck. He took it off and began putting it on everyone's forehead. One by one, the moment his oil-dipped finger touched their heads, they would fall backwards with someone behind them to catch them. They'd then lay them on the floor, and speak frantically to them in tongues.

I remember my head spinning at the sound of hundreds of children, all crying, some shouting, most speaking in tongues throughout that big room.

My turn came. The youth pastor put that oil on his fingertip as I sobbed and cried and readied myself for something to feel—that feeling they kept talking about. I readied myself for my great connection with God. The assistant put his hand on my lower back as the pastor put that oil to my head. He then pushed my head with one hand and with his other on my chest, he spoke: "In the name of JESUS!" They both pushed at the same time, in opposing directions and I fell backwards, just like the others. Only I felt nothing. As I lay on the ground, my eyes opened and I started laughing. It was all just a big show. A spectacle. A recruitment tool preying on minds that weren't even properly developed yet. But the power of suggestion is a helluva thing, ya know?

After that I stopped going to church, stopped worrying about the rapture. I stopped asking God to forgive me of my sins, though not entirely. No, that took some time to break. I had been doing it nearly all my life. Once I became immersed in the world of Punk Rock, I had a recipe for enlightenment.

Freedom.

I saw the church as a mechanism for control. But really, truly, honestly, what did it for me is the fact that in Christianity, homosexuality is a sin punishable by death. Homosexuality is a biological fact, a law of nature, observed in every species of animal on the face of the planet. Yes. Gay dogs, sheep, parrots, sharks, tigers, peacocks, elephants, monkeys, and yes, humans. And, for me, the facts could not be debated or argued. What kind of a god would create a life that was automatically damned? None of it added up, and when I think back on it, it never really did.

At five years old, one of the days I got marched into big church in that Sunday School classroom, I raised my hand, my arm dying from being up so long, "Yes, Daniel?"

"Well . . . what if you lived on an island? Like way out in the middle of the ocean and you never got a chance to know about Jesus. If no missionaries ever came? Would you still go to hell?"

". . . Daniel . . . you know . . . the Lord always has ways of making himself known to all his children of the earth."

"No, but . . . really . . . what if no missionaries ever came? They wouldn't even have Bibles. How would they know about sin? Wouldn't they go to hell?"

The Sunday school teacher looked to her husband (he helped teach the class too) and they shared this strange look on their faces. I remember wondering if they were angry with me.

"Yes, they would go to hell," she said, her lips tightly pressed.

"And what if all the stories in the Bible were just stories? Like the newspapers at the store that talk about Bigfoot. My mommy said those weren't real stories. What if that's what the Bible is and we just think it's real? How do we know?"

It was then that the lady stood up, grabbed my hand, tightened the vice, and walked me down the hall through the double doors and into the big church. She never answered my question so I had to find the answers myself. Thank Elvis I did. Being a Presley-tarian suits me much better.

The Arachnid Next Door

No one believes me;
I can't say I blame them.
It does sound like bullshit.
But it's not.
This is a completely TRUE STORY,
NOT "INSPIRED" BY ANYTHING.

These are the facts:
I was nine years old,
and my sister wasn't quite
three yet,
still a little toddler
when my parents had been
split up for a few months.
We'd stay with Dad on weekends,
then he'd take us back to Mom on
Monday morning,
when he left for work.
Very early.
Before the sun came up.

So one morning,
like other Monday mornings,
as my sister slept in her little car seat,
and I waited for my dad to return to the car,
I started looking around,
like kids do,
when my gaze drifted to
the vacant lot next door.
Dead weeds and shrubs
grew tall there.
I was staring at the lot when suddenly
it appeared
from the darkness
under the yellow street light.
A spider.
A GIANT spider to be exact,

roughly four feet tall
and six feet wide,
including the leg span.
It was tan colored,
with wispy-fine hairs covering its body.
Two rows of shiny black eyes
radiated under the street light
like black diamonds.
Dazzling.
I froze in fear—
just stuck in the moment,
watching this impossible vision
nightmares are made of.
But this was no dream.
This was real.
I watched the spider take
the tall, dry, yellow weeds
into its mouth.
Its fangs worked like a tree chipper,
devouring its breakfast in seconds.
I quickly turned to my sister,
"Kara! Kara! WAKE UP."
But she didn't respond,
just kept snoring in her car seat.
I looked back,
expecting it to be gone,
having vanished into the night,
but it was still there,
eating anything in its path.
I yelled out for my dad.
"Dad! Dad! Dad!"
When I looked back,
the spider was gone.

When I told my dad,
he didn't believe me.
"Boy, you keep lying and the devil gonna
come and take you away in the night.
Feed you to the spider."

That night,
I lay in my bed,
imagining the devil
riding on top of that spider,
galloping to get my ass.

I'm 27 years old now,
and the memory of that spider
stays with me,
crystal clear and
as real as that early morning.
I can't expect you to believe me,
and I can't care whether you do.
I know.
And that's enough for me.
Yeah.
A giant, fuckin' spider.
True story.

The old man always took me to the desert.
It was a part of our lives;
we were always out there
riding three-wheeler ATCs,
taking out the sandrail,
shooting guns.

When I got my first three-wheeler,
a little ATC just for me,
I was seven.
I remember sitting with the idling engine,
my dad buttoning my helmet strap with a snap and
listening intently to what I was being told:
"Now son, LISTEN TO ME, okay? Stay to the trails right here.
DON'T . . . I said DON'T go into the grassy area right there. You
could fall into a hole and really get hurt . . . so BE CAREFUL.
Okay?"
"Okay."
"Alright, go on boy."
"See ya, Dad."
I stuck to the trail for a minute, but
I just had to ride in that field.
It was so much bigger
than my little trail
and I wanted to go fast,
so I turned right into the field.
I could hear my dad start to yell,
but I pushed the throttle faster
and his yelling got louder.
I drowned him out with the sound
of the engine.
Then I felt myself jerk forward
and up
and over
and over again.
I found myself
laying on the yellow-grassed ground,

under heavy rocks,
my hands on the pedals
and my feet under the handlebars.
It was then I saw the cuts on my hands,
the blue and purple skin,
the blood
"Ahhhhhhhhhhhhh!!!" I wailed.
From upside down
I could see the campsite,
my dad running towards me,
his beer tossed to the ground,
pouring out into the dirt.
He got there and pulled the little ATC off me,
throwing it aside like a toy bike.
"Are you okay?" he said, a frenzied look in his eyes.
"I don't knowww . . ." I cried.
His expression was something I'd not seen before.
His look.
He was scared.
He carried me back to our little campsite,
setting me down in the lawn chair he had been sitting in
and began checking my head,
feeling to be sure nothing was broken.
I remember seeing my mom,
her hand over her mouth and her body shaking.
She started snorting and then laughing.
"It's not fuckin' funny, Rhonda! He could be hurt!" the old man
snapped.
"Ha ha ha! I'm sorry! It's jus . . . Danny you threw your fuckin'
beer all the way over there . . . Ha ha ha!"
"It's not funny, Mom!"
"Hey!" my dad said, getting right into my field of vision, his dark
eyes piercing into me, his Budweiser breath right under my nose.
Taking my full attention. "Now what did I tell you? What did I
JUST tell you before you drove off?"
"Not to go in the grassy part . . ."
"Okay, then. See? That's what you get. Now get back on and go
ride . . ."
"But Dad, I don't wanna . . ." I said, still crying.
"Go back on or I'm gonna sell it . . ."
I walked back to the bike, picked it up, and got back on.

I stuck to the trails and went slow.
The old man picked up his empty beer can
and tossed it into the bed of the truck.

He bought a gun just for me,
and sometimes when we were out there
shooting the guns,
we'd stay all day
until I successfully hit a series of targets placed on a big dirt hill—
usually either potatoes or eggs—
with a single-shot .22 Chipmunk.
He trained me well.
I'd hit all the targets
and the old man would smile so big.
And,
on weekends,
entire families would go out there,
everyone shooting in the same direction
side by side
different tailgates,
different guns,
different beers,
different dads
but one common interest.

One day there wasn't anyone else there;
it was just us.
My dad, my tio Gerardo, and me.
We were shooting at targets on the dirt hill
like always,
when I heard gunfire from the other side of the hill.
"GET DOWN!" my dad yelled and I hit the dirt.
Then more shots came,
a whole bunch
whizzing and whipping above my head,
just like in the movies.
My dad returned fire
with me under his arm, as he trotted low.
Gerardo started shooting back too
and we got in the truck.
My dad started it up and made a huge dust cloud,

kicking up a bunch of dirt,
and under it's cover,
we got the hell out of there.

The desert feels like home to me.
I'm comfortable there,
it's honestly the only place I feel human,
like a real person—
a man.
Way out there.
It's not money,
it's not social status,
it's the way it should be—
not my mother or my father's child—
just me.
In my natural state.
Not glued to a screen of one form or another.
No
TV
Phone
Computer
Work
You can actually look up & around
and see nothing but
blue sky, mountains, trees, leaning cacti, animals.
Even the people you're out there with
all seem to shine brighter,
laugh longer, smile more, take bigger breaths,
because
there's less bullshit
than back at home
between our walls
under our roofs
in our little boxes.
The boxes they've put
you
me
and
everyone else into.

We were driving on the road one night,
through the desert
between Ajo & Gila Bend,
a place my dad called
Crater Range.
He told me he saw lots of scary stuff out there.
It was a place where many men had died.
I would stare out the window
into the desert—
the headlights lighting up
the shrubs and rocks;
the full moon in the sky
taking care of the rest:
the arroyos,
the rusty train tracks,
the vast,
never-ending
stretch of white rocks, grasses, and sand—
all illuminated and glowing blue.
And he'd keep talking to me
while my mother and sister slept.
We'd keep talking,
forever it seemed.
I cherished these talks,
the green light in the radio lighting up his face,
his beard moving up and down,
telling me about all the family members & friends
that died on this road.
He told me about them
as we passed through a large formation of rocks
on both sides of the road.
"Class of '79,"
"Martina & Ernesto 4 Ever,"
peace signs & pentagrams
were spray-painted all over the rock walls.
And from that green, glowing radio,
Morrison's voice

singing
about the killer on the road.
And then it'd get real quiet again.
We both would fall into silence,
and I'd just lean my head against that window,
staring out
into the darkness
and looking,
squinting real hard,
looking for something—
anything—
alive and moving,
lit up in the light from the moon
down in the arroyo
or by the tracks.
There was something out there,
I knew it.

THE WHITE CHOLA, SHE NEVER CAME BACK

It was the middle of the school year.
7th grade.
One day a new girl came into
our history class.
Her name was Nicole;
she was just 12 years old,
but she looked 20—
a little girl
in the body of a full-grown woman,
with hips and a big ass in little denim cut-off shorts
and huge tits
under a tight Oakland Raiders' shirt, and
curly brown hair in a white scrunchy.
All the boys were staring,
practically drooling over her.
She wore a lot of makeup
Chola style,
but she still had her eyebrows.
The girl was obviously white . . .
pale skin like a goth doll,
but she talked
like a Mexican girl.
The teacher sat her
right in front of me.
I make friends easily,
so we got to talking.
She said
I was funny and cute.
I was
Johnny-on-the-spot
with the wisecracks.
She had this way of laughing
where she'd throw back her head
and just laugh from her gut,
it was really infectious and cute.

So within a few weeks
I found myself at her house
in Apache Junction.
Our mothers talked
and, beyond all belief,
I was allowed to spend the night at her house.
We mostly just sat in her room
talking,
me watching her mouth move while
nervously thumbing the denim of my pants.
Then that one song came on the radio:
"Kiss me . . . under the blahblhablha"—
repeating those words
"kiss me"
over and over.
We stopped talking and she stared at me
with that look.
The one I know now,
but didn't then.
I just sat there.
Oblivious.
Then she broke her "kiss me" gaze
and started picking up her room.
She talked about this guy a lot.
Some older Mexican guy
named Shorty.
She said he was 22 years old.
Nicole told me about how
this guy used to pick her up in his car,
and they would get drunk and smoke weed.
Just get fucked up and fool around.
She said she put his
dick in her mouth.
"He taught me how to give head. It's not that bad,
except at the end. That part's gross."
I remember thinking
that was really fucking sick.
And I mean
I felt very intimidated.
She was a woman
that did grown-up shit.

I was just a skinny, short kid with a high-pitched voice
and some wisecracks.
I knew I couldn't compete with a 20-year-old Mexican dude
that drove a car
and got his dick sucked.
I didn't even have pubes.
I thought she liked me,
but I could tell
from the tone of her voice
and the way her eyes lit up with fire
when she spoke of that Shorty guy
that she was in love with *him*.
Or at least she thought she was.
She was fucking twelve years old.

That night we made out on the living room floor
while *Saturday Night Live* was on TV.
As she slid her tongue in and out
of my mouth,
I remembered what she said earlier.
Shorty's dick had been in there.
Now my tongue was on the tongue that once
had a dick on it.
The thought made me wanna stop kissing her,
but, of course, I didn't.
Her tattooed biker, twenty-something uncle
sat on the couch behind us,
chuckling to himself and drinking a forty-ounce.
Eventually the dick/mouth thing
left my brain,
and we kissed for that entire episode of *Saturday Night Live*,
a little boner in my JNCO Jeans.
But once *SNL* was over,
she went to bed,
and I fell asleep on the floor.

The following Monday she wasn't at school.
I had a bad feeling,
a sharp pain in my stomach.
I felt it.
When I got home

that afternoon
her mother was at my house
crying and sobbing in my mother's arms on our couch.
They told me she had
run off with Shorty.
But somehow they had gotten a phone number
for where she might be staying.
Her mother called,
but got hung up on every time.
So, for some reason,
they thought I could talk her into coming home.
I had just started drama classes at school
and I remember my mom saying,
"This will have to be your greatest performance ever."
All that drama and shit.
Fuck, Mom, shut up, I thought.
"Hello?" a voice answered.
"What's up, is Nicole there?"
"Who's this?" a male Mexican voice asked.
"Oh, this is her friend Daniel from school. I gotta ask her about homew--"
CLICK.
Her mother just completely lost her shit.
Crying and wailing.
"What if he took her to Mexico
and sold her to a brothel cantina or sex traffickers?"
She had just seen a thing on *60 Minutes*.
Eventually, after she calmed down
and stopped crying,
Nicole's mom said goodbye,
hugging and thanking us both
and she left.
Never saw Nicole again.
I don't know what happened to
that 12-year-old little girl
with the body of a full-grown woman.
All I do know
is that she never came back.

It was a time when everyone was changing. Eighth grade and the boys were becoming men with their voices changing, growth spurts, and hair where there wasn't hair before. *Everyone, besides me* and a handful of other guys I hung with. We were all short, with high-pitched voices—munchkinlike, and pubeless. The girls didn't have any interest in us. But the other lucky bastards were getting laid. I had a friend I hung with, a redheaded kid named Steve. He lived with his mom in the projects. Public housing and shit. Now and then I'd go spend the weekend there. His tiny apartment had no furniture, just beds on the floor. The only thing he had was a TV on a crate and black light with a neon poster.

But we'd leave a lot. Other guys would show up and we'd mess around the apartment complex. Sometimes smoke cigarettes in the attic above the building of the private parking garage for some of the residents. We just moved a painted board in the ceiling and climbed up into the attic. We'd smoke, play cards, and look at porno magazines up there. All by flashlight or we'd light candles. Little tea ones.

"You think it'll ever happen for you?" our friend Randy asked.

"I think so. I got partnered up with Kimberly for that science thing, so maybe."

"Yeah, I heard that girl is pretty fuckin' easy."

"Sharbs told me she fucked Lenny McDonald in a ditch."

"What?"

"Yeah. Seriously. He said that they didn't have a condom, so she just put a plastic grocery bag from the ditch over his dick."

"Hahahaha!"

"AND . . . AND . . . it BROKE! Hahahaha!"

We all just busted up, rolling around on some boards we had put down.

"Lenny was shitting his pants, thinking he knocked her up."

"Be careful, Steve! Ya don't want a grocery bag on your dick!"

That attic was fucking howling with laughter. I guess someone heard us 'cuz some guy's big fucking fat head came poking out of the hole we'd climbed up through.

"Hey, what are you little bastards doing up here?! HUH?"

He scared the shit out of us. Randy especially. I don't know where he thought he was going, but he jumped up and made a break for it. Running. He didn't get too far though. On his third or fourth step he just fuckin' CRASHED through the ceiling. Landing headfirst on someone's car that was parked in one of the garages underneath. The alarm started wailing so loud, we all had to cover our ears. Even Mr. Fathead in the hole. We looked down the hole and it was horrific. The windshield was cracked and smashed with blood and hair all mixed in with the glass. Randy lay crumbled up on the floor. We shouted his name and he began to stir, the alarm was deafening. Slowly he got up, stood/leaned against the car and looked up at Steve and me. A large flap of cloudy skin covered his right eye. Completely. It was bad. Steve screamed at Fathead to call an ambulance.

"Dude? Are you okay?" I asked.

"Of course he's not okay, c'mon man," Steve whispered loudly to me.

"Is your skull cracked at all, dude? C'mon man."

Randy ran his nearly limp hands over his head. Over and over.

"Nahh. Nahh. No, I'm good." He just sat on the hood of the car, staring at the wall. Steve jumped down and wrapped his shirt around his head. He was bleeding a lot. Then Randy spread out on the hood of the car and just passed out. We waited for the ambulance with him. He couldn't be aroused; he was out.

After they loaded him up and we talked to the cops, they walked us back to Steve's mom's. The cops, the dickheads, made us carry the cards, cigarettes, and porno mags right to the front door. Steve and I got grounded for three weeks and Randy got 12 stitches.

My mother kept it from us. I'm glad she did, I would've flipped the fuck out had I known. When I was thirteen, she called me to her room.

"What's up?"

"I want you to hear something." She was going through a box of little cassette tapes.

"What is it, Ma?"

"It's a message someone left on the answering machine back when you were a kid."

"What is it?"

"Just listen." She put the tape into the handheld tape recorder and pushed play.

Just dead air. She rewound it.

"I don't see why ya' can't just tell me."

"Just hold on."

Finally she found it.

A few seconds of silence and then a man's voice. Low and raspy. "Bitch . . . I'm comin' by tonight. And I'm gonna kill you. 187."

And he hung up.

"What the hell, Ma?"

"I didn't wanna scare you and your sister!"

"Why didn't you tell me later?"

"I just did. I came home one day and it was on the machine . . ." She lit a cigarette, her gold bracelets jangling. ". . . so I sent you and your sister to grandma's for the night. Didn't wanna take a chance on anything happening to you guys. Ya know? And . . . I just sat in my bed, against the headboard with my pistol, some Mountain Dew, and a pack of cigarettes. Left all the doors and windows unlocked, sat in the dark and waited until the sun came up."

"Did you get anymore messages on the machine?"

"No. Never again."

"Hmm. It was probably some kids making a prank call."

"I don't think so. Listen to it again."

She pushed rewind and quickly released it. She was right. He sounded older. Dangerous. He sounded like a killer. But then again. What kind of killer calls and leaves a warning message?

Part Two

It was the first time in my life I ever rebelled against anything. I was always a good boy: cautious and courteous. I didn't party or get into trouble at school. I did like my parents asked, always showed respect, came home by curfew and didn't defy them much on anything.

But when I was seventeen years old, a senior in high school, I was introduced to Punk Rock, the standards, the staples: Black Flag, the Misfits, Dead Kennedys, The Ramones, Sex Pistols and one other band that changed my life completely—Minor Threat.

They were a hardcore punk band like others I listened to, but they had something they sang about that caught my attention like nothing else did. It was called "Straight Edge." And it seemed like my kinda thing. Making a stand against drinking, smoking, and doing drugs. I remember hearing the jocks in class bragging about getting wasted and doing stupid shit. Or the burnouts, kids coming into class so stoned they couldn't keep their eyes open. Just seeing and hearing that shit all the time, day in and day out, and hating it, hating them.

With an alcoholic father, it only fueled my fire. "Fuck you, old man, our family's alcoholic legacy ends with you," I said. I was all about it and no one could tell me any different. It was just me and Minor Threat in my room.

I came home from school one day and my mother asks me if I want to get a tattoo. I reminded her that I was only 17, but she said it wasn't a problem. (I later learned that to pay for the tattoo my mom had traded a bottle of pain pills and sixty bucks.) A few hours later I had the words "xStraightEdgex" on my back. I was gonna be this way the rest of my life . . . no doubt about it.

But then Rollins Band came to town, playing an all Black Flag set as a benefit for the West Memphis Three. We nearly shit our plaid pants at the thought of hearing Rollins do those songs. Those songs that meant so much, those songs that got us through the bullshit, those songs that just said it like it was.

So Dr. Ben, Derker, and I went to the show. We walked into the large auditorium of the Marquee and there was the opening band playing on stage. In the pit people were doing shit I'd never seen before. They were punching the air and swinging their arms like windmills, occasionally throwing back a kick. I remember one kid looked like Matt Damon—a little guy with blonde hair and big plugs in his ears throwing spin kicks in the middle of the air like a goddamn ninja. The singer of the band got down from the large and high stage over the barricade and into the crowd. People were dog piling, climbing over each other for a chance to scream words into the microphone. They were all so passionate, just going ape-shit and it looked like they were having a damn good time doing it.

So when I found out that this whole thing was centered around Straight Edge and it was called Hardcore, I knew I had to get into it. I had never been a part of anything and for the first time in my life I wanted to be.

Social networking sites were in their infancy with things like Friendster, Myspace, Livejournal, so I met the entire group of kids that were a part of that crazy display I had seen at the Rollins Band show.

With Dr. Ben and Derker, I went to hang out with them and it was just what we wanted: lighting fireworks in their apartment, singing along to Misfits and Operation Ivy.

We were young, bored, and sober. It didn't take long for me to be accepted into their group. They were welcoming and kind. It felt good to be accepted and wanted by them. They gave me shit—ribbed me 'cause I was a part of the younger group of kids. There were about six of us, new to the scene and wet behind the ears. Then you had the older guys, all in their mid-twenties that played in bands and had their own places.

Just about everybody there was Straight Edge, so we'd have sleepovers, play XBOX, drink big glass bottles of root beer, listen to the Misfits, laugh and crack jokes left and right.

Or we'd go to the busy downtown area of ASU. We had a place we would hang out on Mill Avenue. It was a street corner in front of an Urban Outfitters. We'd stand there, slam dancing & two-stepping, talking shit to people as they walked by, whistling at girls . . . just being obnoxious. But, hey, that's what happened when we hung out on Hardcorner.

But the thing we did most was go to shows. That was what we lived for, waited for—the chance to get all this energy out, to be climbing over dozens of bodies with my friends next to me sweating, screaming, shouting. I had never felt brotherhood with friends like that. We looked out for each other, someone always had your back and you had theirs in return. It could get crazy in the pit, fists and feet flying all around, but if anybody ever got hit or knocked down, there were four people to help them up immediately. We never wanted those nights to end. It was about

unity,

brotherhood,

and respect.

Yet there were things that I chose to ignore, to overlook. But I was aware of them. We were kind of bullies. Everywhere we went it was the intimidation game—puff out your chest and let it be known you weren't to be disrespected. I had never been much of a fighter, usually tried to avoid it at all costs, but now I felt no fear.

Nothing.

I had gotten hit a few times at shows and no longer had that fear of getting into a fight I couldn't get out of. It was nice after being a chubby nerd all throughout high school, getting picked on and just taking it. Fuck no. Not anymore. Even at school, I would outright challenge the jocks and bullies. They'd say, "I'll see you after class." And then I'd be waiting outside, X's drawn in thick black marker on the tops of my hands, a tight t-shirt with "FIGHT ME" stenciled across the front and wearing my brass knuckle belt buckle. They'd always just walk away and it bummed me out. I finally get the balls to stand up for myself and they'd pussy out.

But then shit just got bad. The fun ended pretty quickly. Our once carefree times became something else entirely. We'd be hanging out and one of the older guys would start in on me.

"Danny. Hey, do this . . . do it or I'm gonna fuckin' punch you in the head. Come on."

"What? Fuck you, man. Knock it off," I'd say, trying to watch a YouTube video or some such thing.

"You better do it. One . . . two . . ."

"Dude!"

And then I'd get punched. For nothing. Just because he could. At shows some one of the boys would get into it with someone and start fighting in the pit or outside the venue. But he wasn't even fighting his own fight. Ten seconds into it and there'd be three other kids beating on one other guy. Four on one. I was raised to believe that a man fights his own fight. It's cowardly and there's no honor in it. That's what these kids were supposed to be all about. Honor, respect, and unity.

I remember asking one of them why they'd gang up on people like that and he said, "If one of my brothers is getting his ass kicked, I'm not just gonna stand back and let it happen. I'm gonna have his back and defend my friend."

"But if it's just one guy and it's a fair fight, why interfere? That's his fight to fight, as a man. You win some and you lose some, but you fight it on your own."

Not too many people looked at it the same way.

It just started to be not fun. None of it, so I began to hang out with this guy Donnie and a group he ran with known as "The Black Circle." They were the haven for the rejects of the Hardcore scene. All the disillusioned boys that were sick of the same shit I was. But even though I hung out with beer and whiskey swilling metal heads, I still remained true to my abstinence. I didn't drink. They teased me and gave me shit for it, but they didn't punch me or anything because of it. They respected me enough to leave it alone at a point.

There were still those of us who respected our bodies by being Straight Edge and looked down on those that didn't, yet even among them, I saw numerous guys around me who would stick their dicks into anyone, without a condom and not give a second thought to it.

Of the three "XXX"s in Straight Edge, the last one is supposed to be for sex. The rule being: no casual sex. While some really did/do follow that and stay true to not fucking someone they don't know, there were more that didn't. I even told myself when I first claimed Edge, that I would not fuck anyone that I wasn't in love with. Truth being: I didn't hold true to that at all either. Like getting a blowjob from a drunk chick at a party and not give it a second thought.

One day it just hit me. I was living a lie. I hadn't stayed true to myself. I'd sold out a long time ago. So to make it official I asked my metal head buddy Donnie, as he was standing with a PBR and a smoke: "Donnie. Gimme that beer . . . and that cigarette too."

"No. Danny," he said, his jaw hanging open as I took a swig of beer and a drag from his cigarette coughing it out saying, "This is fun?!"

I got shit from everybody about selling out, but I didn't give a shit. I knew I hadn't been true to myself, so I could no longer claim the XXXs like many others did.

She could never do anything.

Her parents thought nearly everything about her life was either immoral or blasphemous or both.

A boy from school gave her a poster of her favorite band, Good Charlotte, for her birthday.

It was just harmless pop music, but her parents didn't approve of their black clothes, tattoos, spiky hair, and eyeliner.

It was the only thing that hung on her wall that was hers.

Everything else had to do with Joseph Smith & the Mormon Temple. That's all her folks ever talked about, but when she asked questions or was critical of the beliefs of the church, they shut her down with empty answers and irrelevant metaphors.

"But, Mom, there isn't anything bad about this band! It's made for kids!"

"That's what worries me, Amanda . . . the media & music companies want to poison your mind. The morals of this country are falling apart, heck, they're not even there anymore. Amanda . . . you and I both know this band does not follow the teachings of the prophet. You know how we feel, you need to Choose The Right. Remember?"

With her head down and tears falling, she knew she couldn't win. "Yes."

"Okay then," her mom said, tearing the poster off the wall. She then held it out to her. "Come on. Rip it up."

"What?"

"Rip the poster in half."

"No. No way. If you wanna tear it, then you do it. I'm not gonna destroy a gift from my friend. What is the point of this? Am I not allowed to have anything?!"

Her father stormed into the room. "Young lady . . . I am NOT going to stand for such disobedience!"

Her mother stood in the doorway, while her father violently ripped the chords to her phone and TV out of the wall.

"Three months grounding. To your room, no phone, no TV, and absolutely no theater activities after school. I don't care what it's for. Now sit on that bed, and get out your Book of Mormon. Dinner will be ready soon, you can come down then."

He slammed the door shut and locked it from the outside with the special lock they had installed.

She paced the room, her thoughts going a mile a minute.

If she didn't do something, she would lose her mind, she decided. Inside a pile of stuffed animals was a phone. Her secret phone. One of those prepays she kept with babysitting money.

She didn't know if it would do any good, but she called the cops. She had to try something.

An hour later, they were eating dinner in silence when the doorbell rang. Her father shot her a suspicious look before getting up to answer.

The girl could hear the officers talking to her father at the door. They came inside and sat in the den, talking to her parents for a good five minutes, maybe more. Finally, he called her into the room.

"Amanda."

"Yes, Dad."

"Did you call the police on me?"

". . . yes," she said, looking down.

"Why? I haven't hit you. Have I?"

"No. But . . . you keep me locked up all the time. You just won't let me be a normal kid. You're so into the church, you can't see what it's doing to us. Officers, I've spent the past two months locked up in my room. Now they want to ground me three more months. All because I wouldn't tear up a Good Charlotte poster. Just because they're not Mormon, doesn't mean that they're bad. Does everything have to be about church? All the time?!"

The two cops looked at each other, concerned, with wrinkled brows. They were both young. She looked at their crew cuts, blond hair, blue eyes . . . the boys in blue and knew she was doomed, even before they spoke. Finally, one spoke out, clearing his throat.

"Amanda . . . a band like that . . . doesn't follow or honor the teachings of the one, true, prophet . . . Joseph Smith."

"Yes, you really must obey your parents. The Lord commands it," said the other.

"Nooooooooooooo!!!" the girl shrieked all the way up the stairs to her room.

They were everywhere, there was no escape. Her parents, teachers, neighbors, friends, and even the police.

The town belonged to the Mormon church.

She finally embraced the solitude, decided to just ride it out, wait them out and then get out.

When I finally got a car I would drive by her house and she could always be seen there in her bedroom window, frantically waving at me.

She had two long years of that before she was finally granted freedom at eighteen.

My friend in the Tower of Zion, the Mormon Rapunzel, Pretty in Pink with her short blond hair—she had to be free.

Today she lives on a piece of land with her husband and some dogs.

She made it.

Everyone said I was crazy.
   "You'll get arrested."
   "You'll end up stranded in the middle of nowhere."
   "You'll starve."
   "This is how people turn into hobos."
But I couldn't listen to them.
I wouldn't.
This HAD to be done.
My great grandmother had passed down to me an
old suitcase.
A Samsonite from the late fifties.
Not too big, not too small.
It held everything I would need:
two pairs of slacks,
one white belt,
two collared shirts,
one necktie,
three cans of pomade & two combs.
In my bright pink coat,
toting a .38 Special
(a gift from my mother
I'd paid to have customized
with initials TCB
and a lightning bolt pearl handle)
I slung an acoustic guitar over my back,
even though I could only play one song,
"That's Alright Mama."

Scenarios and fantasies ran through my head.
All the colorful characters I'd meet,
all the wild adventures I'd have.
This would be my Great American Odyssey.
The spiritual quest to the American Mecca.
I was going home
to a place I'd never been before.
Standing in the kitchen of my father's house,
I scrawled on a piece of cardboard: MEMPHIS.

Sitting on the suitcase, at the edge of town,
between the confining city
and the vast, open, lonely desert, I
combed my hair—got it high
like The King—
dug my finger into the crevice of my ducktail
and stood up, anticipating the approaching car.
When it passed me,
the gust of wind felt like the heat
of an oven door opening, with your face too close.
The cars kept passing me
all day and into the night.
No one would pick me up.
I waited two whole days in that Arizona sun.
On the third,
I walked back home
and continued the job search.

I used to live with these two friends—a long-haired Navajo guy that was into Satan & death metal and an average white guy into Star Wars & Metallica.

This one night we were going to see Danzig in concert. But before we went to the show, we had to get a money order and mail it to our landlord for rent. The three of us went inside the Circle K, got the money order, cigarettes, and some water.

On the way out, back to the car, sat an old, crusty, homeless Mexican guy, his neck draped in rosaries, like Mr. T is in gold.

As we walked by, he said, "Can you guys spare some change?"

"Sure," my Navajo friend said, digging his pocket for change.

He was just about to drop a handful of change into the bum's hand when the old guy said, "Oh thank you. God bless you . . ."

A smile came over my Navajo friend's face as he put the change back into his pocket.

"Nope. You shouldn't have said that. You just HAD to bring God into it."

"Ohhh fuck you," the old guy yelled.

"Why don't you ask God for some money then?"

We all laughed getting in the car. The old bum kept talking.

"Just get outta here. Something bad is gonna happen to you boys. Go, get away from me. Something bad is gonna happen to you . . ."

"If you don't shut the fuck up, something bad is gonna happen to YOU, motherfucker."

The old man looked down to his rosary and began to pray.

We found an outdoor postal box to mail the money order for the rent. The boys stayed in the car while I got out to mail it. Once at the box, I didn't have a pen to address the envelope. I called out,

"You guys have a pen?"

"Nope."

"Shit."

"Just ask somebody."

I looked up and saw a plump, middle-aged woman getting out of a minivan and head my way.

As we approached each other, I said, "Excuse me? Ma'am? Do you happen to have a pen I could use? I have to send off a money order for rent and I just realized I don't have one . . ."

The lady gave an annoyed sigh, turned back around and walked to her minivan.

I followed.

"I'm sorry to put you out, I just HAVE TO send this out . . ."

Getting into her van, she turned around and screamed at me, "I don't have any money for you to take from me. I WILL NOT BE ACCOSTED."

She started the minivan and made a quick getaway.

"What the hell happened?"

"That crazy broad thought I was trying to rob her."

We all laughed our asses off at her choice of words: ACCOSTED.

So we said fuck it and planned to mail it the next day. The late fee would be $15.00. As we drove off, I remembered the old man's words:

"Something bad is gonna happen." It coulda been worse.

It wasn't quite a party.
More of a kickback.
Just ten or twelve friends
drinking and smoking from a huge glass bong.
All of them huddled around the computer
watching funny YouTube videos
of people getting hurt and shit.
The guy at the controls
went to a website—
ratemyboobs.com or ratemytits.com,
something like that,
and the four girls there
all moaned and groaned,
saying they didn't want to see shit like that.
The guys all laughed
and continued rating the pictures of boobs
as they flashed up one by one,
when all of the sudden
a picture of a guy holding his dick
came up on the screen.
The girls finally had a reason to laugh.
The guys were all grossed out,
but one guy, more than anyone else,
freaked out.
"What the fuck, bro?! I don't wanna see guys' dicks! I'm not gay!"
"Relax man . . . no one said you were. Chill out."
He was hyperventilating and about to
break out in fucking pimples.
"But that's gay shit, bro! I'm not gay,
so I don't wanna see that shit! FUCK!"
He stomped off to the backyard,
lighting a cigarette.
You could still hear him out there
shouting over and over into the dark.
"I'm not gay. I'm not fucking gay!"
he yelled, pacing back & forth.
Everyone around the computer

didn't know what to say,
so they just chuckled quietly
and then one girl said it . . .
what every person there was thinking,
"Wow. That's sad. He's totally gay."
"Yup. Totally gay . . ." the guy at the computer said,
cracking up.
He rated the dick picture
ten out of ten
and moved on
to more tits.

There was something familiar about her face. Something in the way she tossed her brown hair back and smiled. I couldn't quite place it. She was an out-of-town biker bitch. I was just an in-town biker. We leaned against the bar, my hand on her hip.

"Wow. You just don't give a fuck, do you?" she said, wrapping her arms around me.

"Oh, I give a fuck. I'll share it with you, if you want."

Her smile grew wide, as she bit her big, bottom lip. "You wanna get outta here?"

We roared into the motel parking lot on my bike. She pointed to a room, and I parked right next to her bike.

"I say, goddamn. Your bike feels good, makes my thighs twitch," she said.

On the way to the door, her knees trembled. They buckled slightly every few seconds. *Yeah, this was gonna be all right.* Back in the bar, we had something magnetic when we locked eyes. It was always a good sign when you had that. I pushed her down hard on the bed, pressed her mouth to mine. She was a sloppy kisser, all over the place. Not soft and gentle, like I expected. Well, we layed there, kissing and grinding our hips. The chin of my beard was wet.

The radio blared a Doors song.

"Let it roll, baby, roll . . ."

Suddenly, it hit me. *No, no, this is all wrong.* I pulled back.

"What?" she asked, smiling.

"Son of a bitch." I rolled off of her and stood up, tightening the strap of my leather jacket.

"What the fuck?" she shouted, impatiently.

"I can't do this," I said, shaking my head.

"Why the fuck not?"

"Well . . . ugh. You look just like my sister. I couldn't figure it out before, but the resemblance is just too much. Christ, I'm sorry, darlin'."

She sat on the bed, mouth hanging open in disbelief. She slowly formed a sentence.

"Let me get this straight . . . so . . . you're seriously NOT gonna fuck me?"

"Baby, I can't."

"Well, shit," she said, sitting up, pulling her tits back into her AC/DC shirt.

I pulled out a joint and lit it up.

"I can't fuckin' believe this shit . . . lemme hit that."

I passed her the joint.

"Yeah, I know. I can't believe it either. You could be her twin."

"No, it's all right." She took a big hit and held it in as she spoke. "As bad as I wanted to fuck your brains out . . . it's okay. That's actually very respectable. Ya Know? Shows you really care about your family and shit."

"Yeah, I do. Nothin' more important than family."

"You're a good guy, Dan."

"Well, its mainly because I don't wanna feel like I'm fucking my sister."

"Asshole."

She finally passed the joint back.

AN ANGEL FROM HELL ON AN IRON HORSE

On the freeway,
pulling off at my exit,
a big guy in a Hells Angels vest
roars past me,
getting into the turn lane
opposite of my own.
The windows in my '89 mustang are down
with Motorhead blaring out of the shitty speakers,
loud as fuck . . .
the only way to listen to that band.
I stare straight ahead,
avoiding eye contact
with the rebel next to me—
the outsider of society.
He starts to yell at me,
shouting, "HEY!"
over and over
until I finally turn my head,
hoping I hadn't pissed him off,
even in some slight way.
We locked eyes
as the light turned green.
"FUCKIN' MOTORHEAD BROTHER!"
he screamed
revving up and peeling away
as I laughed a sigh of relief.
Guys like that—bikers, nomads,
living in defiance of the law & society,
playing by their rules,
doing whatever the fuck they want,
when they want—
are true symbols of American freedom.
It brings a smile to my face.
But yeah . . .
fuckin' Motorhead brother,
fuckin' Motorhead.

I Am the Passenger, and I Ride and I Ride

A guy riding his bike comes off the curb, and falls into the bike lane on the street. Literally laying in the gutter, his bike on top of him, the wheels spinning in the air. The young man locked eyes with me for a only a second or two. We were both laughing and we both shrugged our shoulders. When shit like that happens, it's all you can do.

—⁂—

For the longest time there was a homeless guy living behind the huge Walgreens' sign at Greenfield & Southern. He had a mattress on the ground, right there, next to the road, behind the sign. Hidden in plain sight. I was amazed the cops didn't make him pack it in right away. For weeks on end, I'd see him there, on his mattress, with his dog.

Every time I drove by, I'd get a quick, three-second glimpse of him. He was like most of the homeless in Mesa—tanned, middle-aged, with graying hair. Usually when I'd get my quick look, passing him, he'd just be sitting with his dog or a fellow homeless friend. But this one time, when I passed, I laughed out loud. The guy behind the sign had a chick on his mattress. A young girl, not homeless by the looks of her. Young, fresh-faced, looked like a cute brunette college girl. They were making out hard and passionately, while one of his homeless friends looked on, grinning wide, watching them suck face. It was a beautiful sight. Everyone deserves a little lovin' from time to time.

—⁂—

As my wife drove around the curve of the 202, we could see it from nearly a mile away, it was up ahead. Glowing in the dark of night. It was a chilling sight, something about flames in the night, on the freeway, made my blood run cold. All the cars ahead slowed down, nearly to a stop, as they passed the car, fully engulfed in flames, just blazing away. The frame of the car all lit up and glowing orange. Firemen were spraying their hoses and trying to get to the door. Someone was still in the car; I could make out the shape of a burning person. With our windows rolled down, we could feel the heat from the raging flames as we passed. We could also hear the screams from inside and smell the burning hair.

—m—

On our way to Phoenix, in our pickup, my mom and I passed through a tunnel. For a five-year-old, it was the coolest thing in the world. The shiny, white tiles all bright with yellow lights. I stared out my window in wide-eyed wonder—the wonder that only kids have.

A little red truck pulled up next to us. Looking down and inside, I saw a man with a woman's head in the driver's lap. But she didn't have any facial features. No nose, mouth, or eyes, just a blank surface. The man was slowly petting the blonde hair of the head. I screamed. My mom looked over and immediately started laughing.

"Don't be scared, mijo . . . it's not real. It's just a mannequin head, like what they put the clothes on in the stores."

"Are you sure, Mom?"

"Yes I'm sure . . . what a fuckin' weirdo though, huh?"

Every time I go through a tunnel with white tiles lit up by yellow lights, I think of this. Even now.

—m—

We were on the freeway, nearly out of Mesa, when the traffic came to a sudden stop. A standstill. Red and blue lights flashed all over. There had been a wreck apparently. As we inched closer, I could see a Harley on the ground, behind a big trailing skid. There were no other vehicles, just the motorcycle. When we passed I saw a big, guy on the ground. The EMTs were pushing down on his chest, performing CPR. With each push, his large belly shook and swayed. Back and forth, back and forth. We finally picked up speed and headed back down the freeway, leaving the red & blue lights behind us. I pulled out my phone and called my father, to be sure it wasn't him. He was all right, at home, but I swear . . . their bellies and bikes coulda been twins.

—m—

. . . a bicycle lying on the sidewalk, next to it, groceries spilled; eggs broken and splattered all over; a gallon of milk split open and pouring into the gutter—a guy sitting between two bushes, his head in his hands, and his body shaking as he sobbed. He looked up at me, red-faced and covered in tears and drool. I stared back, blank as paper.

—ⱳ—

"Jesus fucking Christ! Are you serious? They're still around?" my girlfriend said.

I looked out her window to see the fat couple. Both of them riding one of those "Rascal" scooters. One sat in the seat, the other stood—just cruisin' along together. An overweight parade. We used to see the same two all the time, always around the Gilbert and Broadway area. They'd take turns standing and sitting. One day that guy was standing and steering, with the woman lounging in the chair. The next day they'd reverse positions. Whenever we'd see them, we'd get into a discussion about how lazy Americans are. That, and then the conversation would turn to firebombing the fat scooter couple with a Molotov cocktail. For some reason.

It was a pretty cushy job. I was the parts' delivery driver. I'd get a call over the walkie-talkie, write down what parts were needed, find them in the parts' warehouse tent, load 'em up, and deliver them to the job site. It was pretty easygoing. In between orders I'd just sit in the air-conditioned truck, listening to Howard Stern and napping here and there. When I could. After a month, they hired another guy to be my partner. He was a computer programming geek, married with kids, and he had these stupid cartoon tattoos all over his arms. Japanese anime shit and Hanna-Barbera characters. The guy really got on my nerves, one of those know-it-all nerds.

Our boss was the biggest Native I'd ever seen. Looked like a Navajo Andre the Giant, only he had a big, black, handlebar moustache, which is surprising, because I was under the impression Navajo's couldn't grow facial hair. He stood at nearly 6'6" with long skinny legs and a barrel chest covered in silver and turquoise jewelry. When he got angry, his eyes went wild, like a fire raging out of control. Like the time I got the flatbed truck stuck on an embankment and the back axle snapped off. "GODDAMNIT JUNIOR!" he shouted. My old man was one of the foremen there, so everyone just called me Junior. Oh yes, my boss, Darren, was a scary guy to say the least.

Me and my delivery partner were making a run to the jobsite one day, the radio blaring "Free Bird" by Lynyrd Skynyrd, just getting into the fast final part of the song. The good part. Right in the middle of the guitar solo, my partner changed the station to Nickleback, of all things. I quickly switched it back to the Skynyrd.

"What's wrong with you? Don't change it in the middle of 'Free Bird'," I said.

My partner rolled his eyes and switched it back to Nicklecrap.

"Come on, get with the times, man. This is the new shit."

"Yeah, shit is right."

I switched it back AGAIN, but the song was ending.

"You made me miss the song, ya' fuckin' prick."

"Why don't ya' just cry about it then?"

"Asshole."

We delivered the parts and parked the truck back inside the parts' warehouse tent. With no calls coming in over the radio, we cranked up the a/c and dozed off to Howard Stern talking about an "anal ring toss" game they were going to play. I woke up an hour later to Darren's angry voice coming in over the radio. "Where the fuck are you guys? Goddamnit, we got parts that gotta go out. I'm headed to the tent . . ."

I looked over to my partner, snoring away in the driver's seat. For a second, I contemplated waking him up. Then I remembered the Lynard Skynyrd/Nickleback incident, and I left him sleeping in the truck. I walked out of the tent, to the Porta-John to take a squirt. When I returned to the tent, Darren was staring at my partner, who was still asleep in the truck. Darren's eyes were big and crazy; he was furious. He turned to me.

"What the fuck, Junior?"

"I've been trying to get him up, but he just won't budge. I'm having to do all this work myself!"

"Goddamnit . . ." Darren said, with a heavy sigh, before pounding on the driver's side window.

"Andy! Wake the fuck up, goddamnit! Junior's carrying all the weight here!"

Andy did wake up. He glared at me, and I smiled back with a shit-eating grin.

You don't ever interrupt "The Free Bird."

It was the big *one nine* for me. Nineteenth birthday at Donnie's place. He was throwing a party for me; everyone was gonna be there. Before hardly anyone showed up, we started playing a drinking game—a card game called "Drunk Driver" or "Waterfall" as a few others called it.

"You start at the bottom and flip enough face cards to get to the top. For every non-face you turn over, you gotta gulp down your beer," explained Hustin. He went first to show me how it's done. "You get it?" he asked, chugging down a Natty Ice and twirling a lighter between his fingers, a feat he did often. If it weren't for the massive Japanese tattoos covering him, our friend Hustin or "Seinfeld" as we all called him, looked nearly identical to Jerry Seinfeld. He even talked like him.

"Yeah, yeah, I get it," I said, walking to the bathroom to take a piss. When I returned, the cards were all spread out, face down, and ready for me to play. "Where is everybody? When are they coming, Donnie?"

"Soon. Just play the game."

So, I started playing the game, flipping cards, trying to get to the top. But every card I flipped was a non-face card, so I was guzzling down a lot of beer. Very fast. I never reached the top and pounded down four or five beers before quitting. I had never been drunk before and it hit me fast. A sluggish, tired sadness came over me all at once. I started stumbling around and slurring my words. After a few minutes of standing around, pretending I was okay, the urge to lie down became too strong. I crashed into Donnie's bed. He walked in, laughing at me and shaking his head.

"You all right, Danny?"

"No. No, man. I'm fucked up. Oh god. I'm just like my old man, aren't I Donnie? I'm just like my old man."

"Get a grip, man. You're not like your old man. He's a badass and you're a pussy. Now quit crying and get up." He walked out of the room. I looked to his red digital clock: 7:35 p.m.

I could hear the front door open. Friends were showing up for my 19th birthday party. But I never got up. Just laid there drunk and crying, feeling more like my old man than I ever cared to.

A MATTER OF PRIDE

In line to pay at the gas station,
there's two lines going.
In the line across, at the counter,
stands a big white guy with a shaved head,
the back of his arms tattooed with
"Aryan Pride."
In walks
A short Mexican biker,
body and face covered in old tattoos,
"Brown Pride" on his throat.
Getting in line,
he took off his Locs,
getting a good look at the gringo.
His eyes had those
heavy, deep, grooves—
the hard eyes,
the tired eyes.

"Wanna get ahead of me?"
I asked the Vato biker
with a smile.
He smirked,
"Yeah. I'd appreciate that."
He stepped ahead.
Now flush against the counter
with Aryan Pride,
he stared at him hard.
The big gringo finally
turned and met his eyes.
The staredown
didn't last long at all.
The Mexican-biker guy
was really badass looking.
I don't blame the gringo,
our Mexican friend was the personification
of intimidation.
The gringo held his stare for maybe

four seconds
before looking the other way.
In submission.

It's funny
how primal scenes still play out.
Even within our unnatural urban habitat,
males project dominance,
females protect their young.
We keep fighting it,
telling ourselves
how special we are.
How unique.
But really,
we're just animals, acting out behaviors
and our ultimate nature.
Our true nature
is to destroy ourselves.
The Terminator called it.

"CHECK," SAYS THE WHITE HORSE

I don't know what it is,
but I can always feel when it's coming.
I get this bad feeling
deep in my stomach
and
death's cold hand
on my shoulder.
It's a job he keeps trying to finish,
but I'm always warned.
The gods, the universe, Elvis,
whatever you wanna call it,
have always given me a heads up
before every car wreck.
Every time.

The first accident,
the worst,
was the one that gave me this scar on my face.
I got a heads up on that one—
a big one.
But I ignored it.
When I cranked on the ignition that night,
out of the stereo came
"Storm of Damnation" by Bathory,
an early '80s Black Metal.
The intro track on the first album
is just the sound of waves crashing on an icy beach
and an ominous gonging bell.
That bell ringing, those waves crashing
left my blood ice cold.
I froze up,
couldn't move.
And the scariest thing
was that I had no idea why I was feeling this.
I didn't know what to do with
this icy feeling inside,
telling me,

screaming at me,
DON'T.
But I just chalked it up to being stoned and tired,
so I put in an '80s mix CD,
trying to liven the mood and ease my mind.
But still,
even with Echo & The Bunnymen playing,
the voice inside persisted.
Something wasn't right.
At the red light of Greenfield & University,
that last intersection, just 400 feet from my front door,
the voice said to me, "Run this red light. C'mon! GO! GO! NOW!"
It got so loud, I almost did.
But again, I thought
You're just stoned.
Then, sitting there waiting for the light to change,
a drunk rich boy from the mansions of Red Mountain Ranch
slammed into the back of my truck at over 100 mph,
nearly flattening the bed of my dad's Dodge Ram.
I hit my head on the steering wheel.
I tried to run home, I was so close, I just wanted my mom.
The Chevron clerk ran after me
and told me I was losing a lot of blood,
so I sat on the curb to wait for the ambulance.
My truck sat in a heap of twisted metal.
The rear axle had snapped off and lay in pieces
all over the street.
Sirens approached from all directions.
I ran my fingers across jagged and dangling
pieces of skin,
scratching at my exposed skull
with my fingernail.
Across the street
was the car that hit me,
the front gone,
the engine in the driver's lap.
"This guy looks like he's dyin' over here," someone standing next
to the driver's side door yelled to anyone listening.
"DIE YOU PIECE OF SHIT," I screamed, still touching my skull.
"Hey, take it easy," said a bystander.
"Fuck him, that guy hit me."

74

It didn't seem real.
This first collision
would follow me every day of my life thereafter.
Chonic pain,
a permanent scar,
no money for pain meds, surgery.
I should have listened to my inner premonition,
but I didn't.
I didn't learn from this either.

Seven months later,
I'm at a party,
waiting for my girlfriend and her friend
to pick me up.
My buddy Doyle's girlfriend
had locked herself in the bathroom
and was cutting herself
while Doyle pounded on the door.
My girlfriend showed up,
so I said goodbye
and went outside
to get in her car.
Instantly,
that hand of death
was back again,
but this time,
a boulder dropped into my stomach
and sank all the way down.
"Hey, what's up?" my girlfriend, Amira, asked.
"Fuck . . . we're gonna get in a car wreck tonight . . ."
"Oh, stop it. We are not."
"Okay."
More than anything I wanted out of that car,
but I was buckled in, just along for the ride.
We made a stop by our friend Kathy's house,
picked her up and one other person.
Sandwiched in the back,
Kathy directed us through the Tempe streets
to a house party.
We came to 13th and something
and waited at a red light.

It turned green and we pulled forward into the intersection
when a shitty, white Tracker
made a left, right into the front end of the car.
The back seat jostled
and bounced around real quick,
all of us slamming into each other.
"I TOLD YOU!" I screamed, jumping out of the car.
"Get out of the car!" I yelled at the Mexican dude in the Tracker.
He looked me in the eye,
shrugged, and sped away into the night.

Five months go by and it would strike once more.
That same girlfriend and I—
were now married, with a baby on the way.
In the morning, I was to start a new job, another job.
That night, we were getting ready to watch our shows,
eat some Italian ice,
and then crash out early,
when, whattya know,
that unmistakable
crashing, ice cold, gonging bell
showed itself.
"Fuck."
"What?"
"I'm gonna get in a car wreck tomorrow."
"Oh my god! Stop it with that shit."
"No, baby . . . I can feel it."
She bunched the covers up around her tiny legs
and stared up at me with those giant blue eyes.
"I swear you *will* things into happening.
It's creepy.
Like a really fucked up superpower or something."
"I know . . . it's my gift . . . my curse."
"You're Ghost Rider now?"
"Yes, Amira . . . I am Ghost Rider."
And I tried my best to laugh it off,
even though I still feared for my life.
The next morning
the feeling had only intensified.
I sat sweating and
white-knuckling the wheel

at the metered light to the freeway.
There was one car ahead of me
and I was terrified.
I was sure any second I'd get hit by someone.
And then it came for me.
I *heard* it coming this time too.
That was the worst part.
The sound of it . . .
those screeching tires,
like a runaway train,
headed right at me.
I could see the car
coming up fast behind me.
This was it.
I yelled before the impact.
"Are you fucking shittin' me?!"
It sent the truck slamming into the car in front of me.
I got out of the truck in a rage.
I was gonna unload on this asshole's face.
"GET OUTTA THE FUCKIN' CAR!" I screamed,
pounding on the driver's side door.
A blonde young man got out.
He was in tears,
his hands covering his mouth.
"Danny? Danny, is that you?"
I recognized him immediately.
"Ryan?! Goddamnit! Seriously?!" I asked,
my arms up, my head looking up to the sky.
Ryan was a flamboyant gay guy
I had theater with in high school.
"What the fuck, man?"
"I'm so sorry, Danny . . . oh my god.
My dad is gonna kill me . . ." he said, sobbing.
The truck I was driving was on loan from my grandparents.
Once again it was totaled. A complete loss.
And I lost that job too.

So now, if the feeling ever returns,
I immediately delay whatever I'm doing,
try to throw it off a bit.
My old man taught me that.

He gets these premonitions too.
His moves have gotten him past 50 years,
he must know something
about matters like these.
It's about dodging the white horse
and whipping its ass
with your seat belt cut from the vehicle.

A Dead Boy's Ghost Living in the House

I'd run my finger along
the stitches in my forehead,
look in the mirror
and see my face
still bruised,
black & blue under both eyes
from my face slamming into
that steering wheel.
The rest of my face
swelled up even with the bridge of my nose.
I look like a lion,
I remember thinking.
Laughing at my own reflection
while touching the fresh scar
I was amazed at how numb it felt.
But everything was numb back then,
my whole body.
Every 4 to 6 hours
I'd put on *Friday the 13th Part 6: Jason Lives,*
then as the pills kicked in
I'd pass out,
wake up in the middle of the movie,
nod off again
and wake up just in time for the ending credits.
I wasn't sure I'd ever leave the house again.
Sometimes I'd wake up
to an empty house
and it'd be so quiet
my head would start spinning,
turning,
thinking,
worrying
that
maybe I didn't survive the crash
and this place.
It wasn't my home anymore.
No.

This was purgatory
and I had nothing but time
to think about how close I came
to everything emerging into
blackness and the dreamless sleep.
It felt like it wasn't finished.
I swear to you,
it felt like the grim reaper
was out there,
on the roads
waiting for me.
Eager to collect.

It was the first time I'd ever felt it—that punch to the gut, that knocking the wind outta ya feeling—all from just a look.

Kathy Tequila was throwing a swingin' party, like she always did. I went off exploring the house and opened the door to a bedroom, the smell of weed drawing me in. The door swung open, then bumped to a hard stop.

A pale, pearl-white skinned girl, peeked around the corner. I saw those eyes, those big, blue, exotic eyes mostly only seen from under a veil and I fell completely under her spell.

As she stood there, a lip ring in her hand, the fresh hole in her lip, she said, "Sorry, there's a mirror on the back of the door and I'm trying to put this in. Did you wanna come in?"

She was so tiny—little arms, little hands, with Betty Boop bangs peeking out from under a bandana. She wore a tight Betty Boop ringed t-shirt with a crooked design on the front, a misprint.

She flashed a smile.

I stared at her eyes all done up like one of the Ronnettes.

They had a hypnotic effect on me.

I got shy, like I sometimes do, and told her I didn't need anything. "Sorry."

"Okay . . ." and she closed the door.

Later that night I found myself standing next to her. A yo-yo sat on a table between us.

"Is that your yo-yo?" I asked.

"Hahaha! No . . . why would it be my yo-yo?" she asked, sporting a big smile.

"I dunno. Just askin'. I'm Danny by the way . . ."

"Hi, Danny. I'm Amira."

Six months later I was playing NBA Jam on the Sega with my buddy, Uriah, when the front door opened and she stood in the doorway.

I paused the game and invited her in. This would be my first date with my future ex-wife.

We could talk for hours about anything and everything. It was nice. But sex was truly what bonded us.

The first time we were on the floor of the living room while Uriah read a book in his room. An 80s mix was in the CD player. When "In Your Eyes" by Peter Gabriel started playing, I fell in love. In that moment, with her looking up at me, I saw so much in her eyes. I saw pure beauty, burning churches, sunsets, our unborn child, love. From then on, we were in full-time togetherness, nothing could keep us apart.

My family didn't like her right from the start.

"I just don't like her. Don't have a good feeing about this one."

But I couldn't find anything wrong with her, not at first anyway. It was all just getting stoned together, talking up a storm, chainsmoking, having sex in strange public places, breaking into pools to skinny dip—all the great American teenage kicks.

When I held her in my arms, it was the first time I felt at home with someone, like we belonged together. We fit.

But then the fights started. Stupid teenage bullshit. She'd scream at me and those big eyes took on a whole new life.

What I once saw as intoxicating and beautiful became altogether terrifying. She became agitated and angry. All the time. If she wasn't angry, she was depressed or listless.

I was in love with her and going crazy.

So, to spare myself the round-the-clock heartache, I broke up with her.

It lasted all of one weekend.

Every song at work reminded me of her. "In Your Eyes" must have come on four times that weekend. The night we got back together was when we created our son. We traced it back to that night.

After we got back together, my dad tried to warn me.

"Son, you need to dump that bitch, before you knock her up or something and are stuck with her for the rest of your life. She's nothing but trouble."

And you know what I said?

"Dad. Why don't you mind your own business, alright? I got this."

We had only been dating for four months when we got married at the courthouse. On our wedding night I spent most of it throwing up in the bathroom.

She knew it.

I knew it.

We were going to a party that night. Her period was late. No big deal, it'd been late before.

"Just take this pregnancy test and then we'll go to that party," I told her.

Our friend Kyle was there with us, hanging out, smoking weed & playing guitar.

She had been in the bathroom a while, more than a few minutes, so I opened the door and peeked my head inside. She was standing at the sink with tears in her eyes and the pregnancy test in her hands.

"GET OUT!" she yelled, pushing me out and slamming the door shut.

My blood ran ice cold after that. I rushed to the drugstore to get another test. I had bought the cheapest one earlier, so now I was buying the most expensive one—the one with the little digital read-out, that said: PREGNANT or NOT PREGNANT.

"Everything okay?" the young girl clerk asked.

"Well, I don't know. Looks like I'm about find out," I said with a smirk.

The clerk didn't crack a smile like I expected her too. She just had this blank, grim look on her face and handed me my receipt in silence.

I got back, gave her the fancy digital test and it said the same thing as the cheap one: PREGNANT.

At the time, I was living in a one-room shack in my parents' backyard. Our *little casita*. The three of us just sat in there all night crying and weeping for our youth.

"I can help pay for the abortion if you guys want," our stoner friend Kyle said.

But we decided to keep him. It was a him. And we did the typical thing: we got married at the courthouse with a honeymoon at my parents.

Nothing was the same, everything changed. She never wanted to have a kid and reminded me every chance she got. It wasn't long before she became bitter and hostile.

"This wasn't what I wanted my life to be!" she'd say.

For two and a half years, I lied to myself. *Maybe after she says she loves me, things will be better. Maybe after we get married, things will be better. Once the baby is born, things will be better. Once we get our own place, things will be better.*

But I was waiting for something that was never going to change. She stayed angry and bitter towards me. Everything I did pissed her off. Everything. Just my existence seemed to infuriate her for ruining her body, trapping her into a family she never wanted. There was always a justified reason for her hatred.

Then one day I realized this would be my life until I was dead. So I got out. But neither the hatred, nor the arguments stopped. No. For those first few years after I left, we lived in different places and argued on the phone instead.

Part Three

Another idiot had crashed into me. Totaled the truck my grandparents loaned me. So I had to get a job within walking distance of the house. The baby would be here in just three months. My old man put in a good word for me with the manager of an Osco Drug, just around the corner from my the house. It was so close, I only had to leave five minutes before my shift started. It wasn't bad.

They didn't have an Osco uniform for me, so the lady that drank at the same bar as my old man (a honky-tonk called Roosters) said in her raspy smoker's voice, "We ain't got no uniform for ya', so just take any solid-colored shirt from the aisle. Any one that doesn't have writing on it."

I walked over to the aisle with the hanging shirts and thumbed through dozens of t-shirts with glittery letters, sequins, and plastic jewels that all said "Arizona" and decorated with pictures of Kokopellies, Roadrunners, cacti, and snakes. Then I saw what I needed. A solid, dark denim, collared shirt. I took it from the hanger and changed into it, right there in the middle of the aisle. The manager, Caroline, showed me how to operate the register, and develop film for our one-hour-photo service. Then she left me to it.

The weeks just flew by. Working the evening, closing shift, returning home every night to my parents' house and my new wife, who I'd only known for seven months. She was always in the same place upon my return. Sitting in front of the computer, playing a video game. The kind of game where you build a virtual house, have a virtual family, and go virtual shopping. I thought it was a sad game to play. For some reason.

Back at work, most of the customers came from the senior communities surrounding the area. Old folks playing shuffleboard and Bingo, riding around in golf carts in groups of four, two couple per cart.

I was always most fascinated with the old men's tattoos. A lot of Marine Corp tattoos, usually just one or two on their forearms. Lots of eagles on the Marine Corp tattoos. But one night, this old-timer came in. He was covered in tattoos, up and down his arms. His unbuttoned shirt revealed a large cobra on his chest. His short sleeves were cuffed up to nearly his shoulders, showing off two large, black smears on both arms, near the top. The old-timer's face looked hard and weathered.

"These are some nice tattoos ya' got there, mister. What are those black ones there?"

"Oh, those used to be two black panthers."

"That's really cool."

Most of the old men with tattoos, when I asked them about their tattoos, usually responded with some degree of regret, saying "I got these foolish things when I was in the service, young and dumb. Never shoulda got 'em."

But not this guy, no, he beamed with pride when I asked about 'em. I had just started getting tattoos myself, and I knew then that I wanted to be just like that old-timer with the two large black, smeared panthers. No regrets, he didn't give a fuck. That was so inspiring. Admirable, even.

I can't tell you how many nights I spent on my fifteen-minute break out front, smoking cigarettes and daydreaming. Staring at the senior mobile home park across the street. Thinking of what if Jerry Lee Lewis and his wife came in to vacation here. And they got a place across the street. Jerry Lee might just come in looking for some Dixie Peach pomade for his hair. He'd see what a Cat I was with my greasy pomp and ducktail, and maybe he'd invite me over to have dinner. Play some songs on the piano and let me sing with him.

Then I'd come back to reality and remember Jerry Lee lived on a big ranch house, he'd never come to my hot, dusty, boring, desert town. It was just me at the drugstore and my pregnant, 19-year-old wife on the computer, waiting at home, playing virtual house on the computer and waiting for me to make her cucumber and vinegar sandwiches. The waiting game was never fun. And nobody ever won.

That One Moment (My Billy Holliday)

I had stayed up late that night, smoking a joint in my car after working until 2 a.m. at Applebee's. Around 4 a.m. I finally put my head down and closed my bloodshot eyes. Beyond exhausted.

The moment I closed them, "Danny! Danny! The baby's coming. Danny. Get up! It's time."

"Seriously?!"

"Yes, seriously! Come on, get the bag!"

My mother-in-law asked if I wanted to drive. I was honest, told her about the joint and going to bed late. She just rolled her eyes and told us to get in the car.

They put us in one of the delivery rooms. It was nice in there. Everything looked new and modern, the best.

She had said she wanted to do it naturally, but when those birthing pains kicked in, she was practically begging for drugs. I watched as they put this weird syringe in her back. It was attached to some metal tubing and looked vaguely like something a plumber would use.

The nurses said it would be a few hours and that she should rest before she had to start pushing.

So I kissed her forehead while she lay there scowling at me, and said I was going to get some comics and stuff to read for the long wait ahead.

Atomic Comics was only a mile away. I took my time and ended up with some Walking Dead and Marvel Civil War stuff. When I got back it was nearly time; he was on his way out. I could hear my mother putting up a fit out in the hallway because my wife didn't want my mother in the delivery room.

"Push! Push!" I said and she squeezed my hand so hard it turned white.

The little lady was having trouble getting him out, so they cut her to give him more room.

"He's crowning. Wanna see, Dad?"

"Don't look! I want my vagina to stay beautiful to you."

But I ignored her and took a look anyway.

Blood, juices, and a little tiny head. Lots of thick black hair. I reached out and touched him gently. He was nearly out. And with a few more pushes, out he came. Liquid splattered and pattered to the tiled floor.

"Let me hold my baby," she said

"Just hold on, Mom. We've got to clean him off and warm him up."

I cut the umbilical cord and stepped aside while they finished cleaning him off. He was beautiful. I had been thinking of nothing, but this moment for nine months. What would he look like? How would he sound? Who would he be?

When she was pregnant we had this little device. It was a microphone/headphone set so you could listen to the baby. But I didn't use it for that. I played Elvis Presley for him nightly and spoke to him all the time. I wanted him to know my voice.

When they were finally done cleaning him, they placed him under a heated lamp.

He kept screaming until I began talking to him.

"Hey there little man. It's me pal, it's your Dad."

He stopped screaming and focused his little eyes on mine. We just stared at each other in wonder. In that one moment everything changed and nothing has ever been the same. Especially for me.

Now he's this skinny, goofy, kid.

He's in his room right now playing an Indiana Jones videogame and shouting, "DAD! I NEED YOUR HELP! I CAN'T BEAT THESE GERMANS . . . DAD!"

So I'd better get going. Goddamn Nazis.

Mi Familia

After our son was born,
that first night,
when it was just the three of us
laying in the hospital bed of the maternity ward
looking at our little guy
all wrapped up and
yawning a big one,
my wife and I both laughing
at how unbelievably cute he was
doing the simplest little things—
yawning, sneezing, making faces,
looking all around the room
with those big brown eyes,
I remember
her getting so upset
because everyone kept saying
how much he looked just like me
and not her.
"No baby. Look at him.
Yeah, he's got my brown eyes, sure,
but look at how big they are! That's all you,
so don't worry darlin' . . . he looks like you too."
The day after he was born
she sent me back to the house
to grab a few things we forgot
in our rush to get to the hospital.
She asked me to hurry back
and I told her I would.
"Just in and out," I said.
At this point
I had been awake for over 48 hours straight.
Hadn't slept a wink
that first night in the maternity ward.
Stayed up
staring
at my perfect, healthy, baby boy
and my beautiful wife.

So after I gathered up
all the stuff at the house,
I laid my head down on our bed.
I was only going to rest my eyes.
Sincerely, I was.
I woke up four hours later
to the sound of my phone vibrating next to my head.
"Where are you?!" my wife screamed, in tears.
"I'm so sorry baby, I fell asleep. But, I'm on my way!"
It took her a while to calm down,
but eventually she did.
We ate banana pudding with whipped cream,
and Nilla wafers
and laughed at
our little, yawning Billy Holliday.
Everything was right with the world.
I was a man with a family all my own.
That was before the storm and the hard rains came.
I wouldn't have that peacefulness for long.
But while I did,
in those early days,
with just the three of us,
it was the greatest of times.
I have never known such happiness.
Before or since.

It was the summer of the serial killers in Arizona. You had the Baseline Rapist, who was raping and killing women all up and down Baseline Road. And in my hometown of Mesa, two men were randomly shooting and killing people, week after week. People out walking, jogging, or sitting leisurely outside were gunned down. The streets were extra hot that summer and no one felt safe.

The baby had been born only a few months before and we were staying at my in-law's house. Just about every night, my buddy Monty would come over, and we'd sit in his car, smoke weed and share new music with each other. One night, we're doing just that, in front of my mother-in-law's house. N.W.A.'s *Straight Outta Compton* album bumped and rattled the speakers of Monty's little Dodge Neon as we passed a joint back and forth. Since I was a boy, my dad had always told me, "Be aware of your surroundings. At all times." It stuck. I noticed one of the neighbors drive by, staring long and hard at us as he slowly passed. A minute later, the car drove by again and did the same thing.

"Shit. I think someone saw us."

"What?"

"Yeah, some neighbor just drove by. Twice. Staring at us."

"Nah, it's all good, man. You're just being . . . how you say . . . paranoi?" he said in his best Tony Montana.

"No seriously, man. I think we should put this shit out," I said, passing the joint back to him.

"You're just stoned, pal. It's nothing."

Not more than five minutes later, an SUV pulled to the curb, across the street. The joint was smoldering in the ashtray, a little roach was all that was left.

"Fuck. Light up a cigarette and get out of the car, quick," I said, in a panic.

"That's not a cop, dude."

"YES, it IS. It's a sheriff's SUV! GET OUT! Don't let too much smoke out." We quickly sparked up two cigarettes and exited the car. We saw the sheriff walking across the street, right to us.

"Okay, you just found out your baby's mama is suing you for full custody, you're upset, and we were talking," I said as quickly as I could. It was the truth too.

"Good evening. What you fellas up to?" As he approached he turned down his radio.

"Nothing. Just talking, smoking cigarettes," I answered.

"Talking, huh?"

"Yeah. My baby's mama is suing for full custody. I was upset, so I came over to talk," Monty said, doing that nervous thing with his thumb on his jeans.

"Oh, damn, that sucks. Sorry to hear that," said the sheriff studying our IDs as we handed them over. We knew the routine. He stood silent, looking at them, tapping them against the palm of his hand.

"Alright, guys. Let me run these. If all comes back okay, you're all right.

"Okay."

"Just hang tight," he said, walking off to his vehicle.

I looked behind me to Monty's car. Smoke from the joint danced and whirled inside, swirling around, just waiting to be let out. If that door opened, our fates would be sealed.

"Fuck, man. We're screwed, we're so fuckin' screwed," Monty said, lighting yet another cigarette.

"No we're not, no we're not. Just keep talking about our kids, play that up. We'll be fine. You know this guy's got kids too. It's our best shot. We got this, man."

The sheriff, in his black boots, clomped back across the street to us. "Alright, Mr. Valdez, here ya' go." He handed me my license.

"Thank you."

"And this is your house?" The sheriff pointed towards the house.

"My mother-in-law's, yeah. My wife and I just had a baby."

"Oh yeah? Boy or girl?"

"Boy."

The sheriff smiled and made a thumbs up, like "right on." I nervously gave a thumbs up back.

"Now you . . ." He turned to Monty. ". . . you actually have a suspended license. Did you know that?"

"What? No, I had NO idea."

"Yeah. Now . . . is there anything in the car . . . anything I should know about?" He reached for the door handle on the driver's side.

"No, not at all, officer."

"No drugs? No weapons? Right?"

"No nothing like that."

"Okay," he said, taking his hand off the handle and scribbling something on a clipboard. "But I am gonna have to cite you. Your registration is expired. He tore off a ticket and handed it to Monty.

"Yes. Of course."

"And just be careful out here. The reason we came out here tonight was 'cause some one reported seeing two suspicious men in a vehicle."

"Oh, yeah! What with all the killings going on . . . I don't blame them."

"Yeah. So you guys be safe and stay out of trouble."

"We will," we both said in unison, a little too enthusiastically.

"Oh! And GOOD LUCK with your baby's mama! I got an ex-wife, too, know how that goes. Have a good night!" He started up and pulled away.

We couldn't stop laughing at our good fortune. We came too close to going to jail. We switched to Track 2 on the *Straight Outta Compton* CD, turned it up and lit another joint. It was an extra hot summer that year.

THE MAN IN THE ATTIC

To this day
I still can't explain it.
That's what makes it
all the more terrifying.
My wife and I had just moved into
our first apartment together
with our seven-month-old son.
The complex was small,
only twelve units in all and
built in the early 1960s.
One night we were sleeping in our bed
with our infant son in between us.
We both woke up to a loud thud sound
and looked to see our son crying from the floor
at the foot of the bed.
My wife sprang up out and scooped him up.
"Oh my God. Did I just dream that or--no--no."
"What? What happpened"
"Danny . . . I swear . . .
someone picked Billy up
and when I woke up they dropped him . . .
and went back in there."
She pointed to the pitch-black doorway
of the closet.
The door was wide open
and infinitely dark.
I got up and turned on the light.
The closet was empty
except for the hanging clothes.
"Are you sure, it wasn't a dream?"
"I'm pretty sure."
In the closet was a door in the ceiling.
I'd never noticed it until that moment, that night.
We were on the second floor
of a two-level apartment building.
I didn't know apartments could have attics.
But, then again, this place was over forty years old.

I put a chair from the kitchen in the closet
and stood atop it,
and lifted up the little attic door.
I hoisted myself up with a flashlight in hand,
while my wife & son
sat on the bed, watching.
Shining the light around I saw
food wrappers, dead mice,
and empty bottles of liquor and water.
But the scary thing was,
I could see now
that all the apartments in this complex
were connected by this attic.
Shining the light over,
I could see my neighbors' attic doors
which led straight down into their closets
and with the turn of a knob into their bedrooms.
But I didn't see anyone up there.
I didn't hear anything.
I just felt the darkness and the silence.
After closing up the attic door
and getting back in bed,
we were unable to fall back asleep.
But that was nothing—
that was just how it started.
The following night
we had a couple friends over.
We sat around, smoked and talked
just like we always did.
I was right the middle of a story
when everyone froze up
and stared at the ceiling,
at the sound of running footsteps
all along the ceiling,
moving from the kitchen to the living room,
and back again.
The room became grimly silent
as my wife and I looked to each other,
our faces sheet white and drenched in fear.
"What . . . the . . . fuck?" someone said.

Once again, it was really hard to get to sleep that night,
even though we were so tired.
Finally I moved the baby's changing table
in front of the closet door.
I can't count how many nights after that I'd be alone in the dark,
watching TV in the living room,
when the running footsteps would start up.
Every time it would happen,
with those first steps I'd hear,
my blood would run cold as ice
and my entire body would tense up.
Sometimes it would go on for minutes at a time.
Just running
back and forth,
back and forth.
After a few months
the footsteps finally stopped.
But we never did find out
what or who it was
running on the ceiling
and paralyzing us with fear—
That man in the attic.

There were many times when I came close to leaving. I would take some clothes and my favorite movies with me to my parents' house, dead set on not going back. But then she would come over and talk me out of it.

When it finally happened, though, this is how it went down:

It was the Fourth of July and I was driving home from my job at a group home for the developmentally disabled, fireworks bursting all around me up in the Arizona sky. I was caught up in a full-blown panic attack from the thought of my twelve-hour shift the next day with no pain pills or any relief whatsoever. I had a severe back injury from a car wreck and that day I had hurt it worse moving someone from wheelchair to shower. It felt like a railroad spike had been rammed into the center of my spine. Driving home, then walking up the stairs to our apartment—I couldn't stop crying. I had lost all control. Walking in the front door, my wife was cooking and my son crawled on the floor. I went straight to the bathroom, to calm down and compose myself, but I just couldn't stop crying. Hell, I couldn't even catch my breath. My wife walked in.

"What's wrong? Why are you cryin'?"

"I hurt my back really bad today at work . . . and I have a twelve-hour shift tomorrow and no pain pills, no nothing. It just hurts so bad . . ."

She rolled her big blue eyes, eyes once beautiful to me, and scoffed at me.

"That's no reason to be fucking crying. Quit being a baby."

Out the door she went with a slam. THAT was my wife? My true love? The one I was to be with until death?

I ate dinner in silence, put the baby to bed and smoked so much weed, I felt nothing, neither physical nor mental. I couldn't smoke weed before or at work, however. I did have morals. Those people were my responsibility.

The baby woke up crying around five a.m., and I had to start my shift at eight a.m. It was the wife's day off.

"Hey . . . hey . . . wake up. Can you get him? Please?"

"Arrgg. No. Just get up with him." She groaned and rolled back over.

"Please? I gotta be up in two hours."

"Ugh. NO. It's my day off."

"Exactly. You can take a nap with him later. I gotta work twelve hours today."

"I said NO. I didn't want a baby in the first place. Remember?" She said that all the time. It made my blood fuckin' boil.

"Then maybe you should've kept your fucking legs closed."

The baby kept crying, screaming, now a blood-curdling sound. The next thing I saw were flashes of red, black, and white as her small, but boney, rock hard fist hit the side of my temple.

"YOU FUCKIN' CUNT," I screamed jumping up and out of bed. Picking the baby up, he rested his little head on my shoulder, and finally stopped crying. I walked the floor, pacing back and forth, my back aching, my head throbbing and pulsating as the goose-egg lump swelled.

She sat upright in bed. Her arms crossed, her fierce glare burning a hole through my head. She didn't look the same anymore. Her past beauty replaced instead with little saggy titties and wiry, stringy mess of hair—like a Barbie doll left outside too long. And that face. My God, that face of hers. She hated me. Everything I did and said pissed her off.

Holding my son, I stood at the bedroom window and watched in envy as the cars moved so freely along the street. I recalled the fights, all the shiners, lumps, goose-eggs, cuts, and bruises she had left on me over the past nine months. Where she once looked at me with those big blue eyes, there was love, lust, and a future; now it was hate, hate, hate, and a wasted life. I thought of all this while watching those cars travel down the street when it suddenly became clear to me, I could be in one of those cars too. Driving somewhere, anywhere, far from her.

I kissed my son, put him on the bed and went into the closet, and started grabbing my shit.

"No, no, no, no. You can't leave. You CAN'T." She started to panic.

"Watch me. This is it, you hateful bitch. Get out of my way."

She ran behind me, followed me down the stairs, all the way to the car, shrieking, screaming continuously, and slobbering and gasping for air, throwing herself in my path. Tears flowed from her oversized eyes, now filled with tiny red veins.

"We can go to counseling; we can work it out."

"I don't WANT to work it out. I don't love you anymore. Now would you get back upstairs? You left the baby all by himself up there."

She didn't hear me. Just kept on trying to convince me. I managed to get my clothes in the car, but then she wouldn't let me close my door.

"I can't believe this. I can't believe you. You're just leaving your child?"

"No. I'm leaving YOU. Now get back upstairs and be a mother. You're done being a wife."

I had to pry her claws off the driver's side door to leave. Looking in the rearview I saw her skinny body running up the stairs, back to our apartment and the baby.

My first meal as a free man was an egg & cheese biscuit. I sat in my parked car in the parking lot of a park, listening to my iPod on shuffle.

"Don't Think Twice, It's All Right" by Bob Dylan came on.

I took it as a sign.

Living Free & Not Givin' a Shit

I didn't know it, but
the night before
a scorpion had stung me.
I didn't realize it until I was already at work.
A big & swollen, red bump materialized on my leg.
It fucking burned.
I got permission to leave early
from my lesbian, man-hating boss.
"And you can't come back to work, unless you get a doctor's note,"
she shouted down the hall
as I walked out.
Driving home through Old-Town Gilbert,
right on Gilbert Road,
I could hear sirens.
A lot of them
ringing over the Link Wray coming out my speakers.
Everyone pulled over,
including me.
From what I could see,
the cops were chasing someone
at a slow speed.
A shitty, ghetto-fab, grey '70s Cadillac
led the way . . .
a dozen black & white squad cars
right on his ass.
When the fugitive drove past me,
he was in the center lane.
We made eye contact.
Really locked eyes.
A large, Tongan guy
with poofy hair and a cigar dangling from his mouth.
When he passed me,
he smiled big, raised his eyebrows, and
gave me a wink with his eye.
Then he accelerated,
blew through a red light
and made a wild right turn.

Out of sight
and roaring away.
A week later,
I'm at the grocery store
and who do I see?
The fugitive Tongan guy.
I'm sure it was him
because
he was still smiling
the smile of a free man.
When he saw me
his eyes lit up
and
as I passed him
in the cereal aisle,
he winked at me
and we both burst into laughter.
I had to shake his hand.
He was the man.
The man that outran
the man.
An American hero in my eyes—
living free and not giving a shit
what this country is all about.

In the past ten years the world has changed completely. The Digital Age. That's what they all call it. You used to be able to fill out a paper application, hand it to the manager and begin to charm your way in. No. Not in the digital age. Everything is done online. Face-to-face is dead. And everyone—the people out there in the world—the people in markets, shopping malls, restaurants, bars and cafes, everyone, they've all got their heads down, their faces illuminated, their thumbs working a mile a minute. They're everywhere. A table at a pizzeria, with an entire family there eating: Mom, Dad, the two teenage girls, and the ten year-old boy—they've all got devices in their hands and faces lit up. No one talks to each other, except to share a funny video occasionally.

We're all becoming strangers to each other. Putting all of our eggs into one digital basket—phone numbers, addresses, credit card numbers, social security information, passwords, every conversation, every call, every move we make, what kind of foods we eat, what books we read (or don't), what political causes we support, pictures of our kids, families, homes, naked lovers—it's all on one little device. Paper is a sin, didn't ya hear? Ya gotta go green, go digital, you're either with us or against us. It's a dangerous game the world is getting itself into—a real house of cards. A mansion built on a sand cliff, sharing a bank account with a junkie.

All it would take is for the satellites to get shut off, damaged, knocked out, wiped out.

Don't laugh like that. Don't brush it off. Don't be so smug.

It could happen. This way of life is not untouchable.

What will you do when the apps won't load? When your devices no longer sync to the network? When there is no page to display and everyone is left with zero bars and no signal?

When then? When the digital age becomes the Dark Age.

What then?

Huh?

You fucks.

Part Four

The Pits (Death in the Streets)

There's death in the streets.
Believe me.
I've seen it.
On a walk to the grocery store
I saw it.
I went into the store,
came back out,
and there they were,
spread out all over:
Two old gals
from the senior apartments across the street.
One was split in half
at the waist.
The other was ripped open at the stomach,
her insides
spread about and ground into the black asphalt
like silly string the night after a big party.
There were other pieces of the old gals too.
Something green and something brown,
glossy and shining in the sun.
(Reminded me of when my dad and I
once gutted an elk.)
Four people died in that spot
over a few years,
until they finally
put in a crosswalk and a light.

In downtown Phoenix
I was out job hunting
and I saw a guy standing at the bus stop
across the street, where I was going to catch the bus.
He looked like Chris Farley
in that "Da Bears" SNL sketch.
Moustache, blue blocker sunglasses, the whole getup.
By the time I crossed the street,
he was on his back
on the sidewalk,

his limbs spread out.
People—
3 or 4 of them—
stood over him.
Someone was on their phone
calling 911.
The bench at the stop was empty, so I took a seat
to watch everyone else panic.
I didn't bother standing over him too.
What was I gonna do?
Some bitch started shouting:
"OH MY GOD! HE'S DYING! HE'S DYING!"
I stood up on the bench
and looked over the shoulders of everyone
down at the guy
while he took his last breaths,
gasping in air,
getting slower and slower,
his jaw jerking up and down.
He died.
Right there.
By the time the EMTs showed up,
he had been dead five minutes.
They tried to shut his eyes,
but this wasn't a fucking movie,
so they wouldn't close.
He lay fixed, just staring up into the sky.
My bus pulled up
as they were loading his body up.
For some reason,
that one really got to me.
More than the splattered old ladies even.
It just seemed so shitty to me.
Dying at the bus stop,
taking your last breath,
knowing that you never got anywhere.
That'd be the pits.

Family Curses

It was the damnedest thing.
My old man had warned me about it
when I was a fat, awkward teenager,
thinking I'd never land a chick.
He warned me I would and it would create more problems
than I'd ever dreamed.
"The Valdez Curse"
is what he always called it.

My pals and I would be out
in the bars,
on the patios,
drinking and smoking,
talking up a storm with everyone.
They'd start in on a chick,
strike up a conversation,
spitting game at her
and the chicks knew . . .
they always knew
what we were doing,
what we were after.
That's why I could never do it.
I couldn't just stroll up to a lady
and start in on her.
What was I gonna say?
"Hi, I'm Danny. I'm unemployed, I live at my father's house."
No.
So I'd just stand there,
keeping to myself,
sipping my water,
pondering the next cigarette.
But I was pretty lucky.
Someone would wind up talking to me.
Some girl, some woman,
would start in on me.
If I played my cards right
or if the electricity was there,

I'd go home with her.
My buddies couldn't help but get pissed off a little bit,
"You don't have a car,
you don't have no fuckin' money, and yet . . .
you can still get a chick to just take you home.
I love ya man, but goddamnit,
fuck you."
Turns out my old man's friends said the same shit
to him,
when he was 22 years old.
The Valdez Curse.

BEDROOM ATHLETE

Donnie said it was a bachelor/bachelorette party
being held simultaneously
in the same house.
The ladies in the den
and the guys in the living room.
It didn't get very far
before a fight broke out.
The groom hit the bride
for having a dick wagged in her face.
The house erupted in chaos,
people running in all directions,
snatching up booze
and backpacks filled with PBR.
I caught a ride with this chick—
a real curvy lady with big, hanging tits.
She was in our partying circle.
This lady was a part of a group of girls
that did whatever the fuck they pleased,
and made no apologies.
They listened to "Peaches" a lot,
you know,
a lively pack of females.
We ended up back at Donnie's,
everyone else was gone
off to another party,
so we were all alone.

Bursting through the door
of Scotty-Too-Hotty's room,
we got naked as fast as we could,
fell to the floor and started to make it.
The combination of being so drunk,
not having gotten laid for a few weeks,
and her pale flesh-pillows shaking back & forth,
turned me into a two-pump chump.
It was pathetic.
The worse performance of my dick's entire career.

Literally ten seconds,
and I was done.
I couldn't help it, but
the laughter just came pouring out of me.
"Are you fucking kidding me?! Uh-uh.
No fuckin' way . . ." she yelled.
"I'm sorry. I uh . . . I uh . . . ha ha ha!
I'm gonna go watch *The Lost Boys*."
"You fuckin' asshole."
"I'm sorry. We could go again. I could last longer now."
"No we can't. I don't have anymore condoms. Do you?"
"No."
"Okay then," she said, putting her tits into her bra.

Word spread quickly.
By Saturday night
everyone knew.
It was the comedic relief of the weekend.
In her gang of girls
there was one, in particular—
a chick I thought carried herself very well,
she walked with swag and she had class,
everybody called her Smashly—
I had always been trying to get with her.
We partied and hung out in the same group
almost every weekend.
I was always trying,
but she was never having it.
I got shot down every time.
After this two-pump incident,
any chances I thought might still remain,
vanished in a mushroom cloud.
She gave me the most shit
out of all the girls.
I pleaded my case,
explained that I was a victim of circumstance
and how I normally had very high stamina in the bedroom.

We were at a party one night
and I saw a friend with benefits I used to have.
We got to talking and like an asshole,

I had her tell Smashly that I was alright.
But everyone just laughed
and called me a two-pump chump,
a premature ejaculator,
like the old song goes.

And it was the damnedest thing,
but a couple of years later,
I get a random message from Smashly,
asking me if I wanna come to a little kickback at her place.
When I got there,
it was the usual suspects—
all of the Monster Squad Party Crew,
about 7 or 8 of us.
We drank and smoked weed,
laughing about old times
and getting silly.
Then all at once,
everyone started talking about having to get up early,
and the fake yawns started.
They were all looking at each other and laughing.
The guys were patting me on the back,
with big shit-eating grins saying,
"Dude . . . I think you're gonna have a good night.
I'll see ya later."
"Alright you two . . . have fun.
Don't do anything I wouldn't do, Danny boy!"
And the door slammed shut.
She locked it and turned around to me.
I had a smirk on my face.
I couldn't believe I didn't know what this was from the start.
It was funny.
We sat on the couch and made with the small talk,
and then she just spit it all out.
"So . . . yeah. Let's see what you got."
We did everything two people can do
without getting too kinky.
Even I was impressed by how long
I lasted—
Forty-five minutes, nearly an hour—
I figured then, that I'd go down on her a bit,

then go back to fucking and finish her off.
When I crawled down to assume the position,
I noticed a tattoo
just above her pubic area,
it was something in French.
"What's this say?"
"Lire sur mes lèvres . . . it means 'read my lips'."
I chuckled and got to work.
See that's what I mean . . .
that woman had some class.
When she came
her legs clamped on my head, covering my ears.
I couldn't hear anything but her muffled moans.
Her muscles relaxed,
and then she slowly released her death grip.
She let out a big sigh and got up.
Walking to the bathroom, she said,
"Whew . . . well . . . good job."
"Are we gonna keep going? I haven't come yet . . ."
She laughed at me. "No."

I walked across the street to my buddy's house,
entered the living room to
blue and glowing rays from the TV screen.
Everyone sprawled out,
stoned and dozing on the couch.
I sat on the couch for, maybe, one minute
before rushing to the bathroom
to rub one out and finish myself off.
And even though that night ended in me
jerking off in a sink,
it felt like
hitting a home run over the stadium wall,
finding a hundred dollar bill in the gutter,
having Motorhead play your house party.
More than anything,
I was just happy to be good at something.

Bottom of the Barrel, Top of the Heap

After leaving my wife and
blowing through all my settlement money
from the wreck that left me with my scar,
I was down & out.
My best friend Monty and I got evicted from our apartment
and I ended up back at my father's house.
I had it all—
a car
a job
an apartment
an envelope full of one hundred dollar bills.
But that all
came to a screeching halt
and this new life began.
December of 2007.
For the first time in my life
I was put face to face
with the person I'd been running from
and trying to avoid the most,
myself.
Most people can't handle being isolated and alone
24 hours a day,
7 days a week,
for weeks on end.
But I had no other choice.
With no phone, computer, television, money or transportation
it was just me, myself, and I.
At first I was just cursing myself
for blowing all my money,
losing my car/driver's license,
and getting fired from my job at the group home.
The worst part being, that it was no one's fault
but mine
and now I had to pay the price.
And pay it I would.
I learned a lot about who I was
and what made me tick.

I had a nice suit,
perfectly combed hair,
new tattoos,
a big screen HDTV,
but not a dollar to my name or a friend to call upon.
I tried to get out as much as I could.
After two weeks straight of total isolation,
I couldn't bear to just sit in that house anymore,
from sunrise to sunset.
It was driving me to the brink of madness.
So I pounded the pavement,
put in applications,
and tried to find work.
It was a brutal two weeks
of walking the dusty streets
in my small desert town,
spread apart by miles and miles
of desert and abandoned shopping centers,
applying anywhere and everywhere.
But after two weeks,
I still had nothing.
Christmas came and went
and it was just before New Year's Eve
that I finally knew what I had to do.
There was a fifties-themed diner
up by the mall.
I knew I could get a job there as a server.
I had serving experience,
and picture perfect Elvis Presley-grade hair.
I knew it was a sure thing.
So I combed my hair right,
pomped it up high,
put on a pink-collared shirt,
black suit coat,
slacks,
and my blue suede shoes.
I walked in and the waitress standing at the counter
did a double take.
Her eyes, dark and smoldering,
sorta like Lisa Marie Presley's,
practically peeled my clothes off.

116

with her eyes,
So I hammed it up,
"Hey there, darlin'. Can I get an application?"
"Yeah! Of course! Let me get the manager."
And she ran off,
her hips moving up and down
in that cute little black & white '50s dress.
She came back out a minute later,
"Okay, she's on her way out. So what's your name?"
"I'm Danny."
"Ha ha ha! Like Danny Zuko!"
"Yeah, I reckon. What's your name pretty lady?" I asked,
flashing a half-smile.
"I'm Ashley."
When the manager came out
she asked if I had served before.
I told her I had and gave her the details.
The next question was just what I was hoping for—
"When can you start?"
And just like that,
everything changed.
The solitude of the winter of '07
had finally come to an end.
From then on
it was milkshakes,
grilled cheese sandwiches with pickles and fries.
I filled up the jukebox with CDs from my vast music collection,
got stoned and had sex
with the waitress Ashley,
spending my own pocket change to hear
Gene Vincent or Buddy Holly
boom throughout that '50s diner.
It was unbelievable how quickly everything turned around for me.
So the next time you think
things can't get any better
and you're stuck living in your own personal hell,
don't worry,
because, in the span of just one day,
you can wake up at the bottom of the barrel
and go to sleep at the top of the heap.

THE SUPERSTITION DINER

I was like a rooster in a hen house.
Besides the cooks in the back,
the teenage bus boys,
and the Mexican dishwashers,
I was the only male employee there.
The only guy server in the entire diner.
Just me and dozens of ladies.
I never stopped smiling in those days.
In my first few days,
I heard lots of whispers
and rumors
about which waitresses thought I was cute
or whatever.
Most of the talk I heard
was about these two girls in particular.
One named Raven,
a petite white girl, with blue eyes and blonde hair.
Really feisty and sarcastic, a real gas to be around.
The other was
the waitress I met when I came in to apply.
Ashley.
She was eighteen, with brown hair, nice curves, and of course
those smoldering, dark eyes that first got my attention.
They were both sexy,
and I couldn't really choose one over the other.
They both invited me over
to Sarah's house
for a New Year's Eve block party.
I didn't know what was gonna happen.
But that night at the party
Raven brought with her
an ex-girlfriend and it looked like I was
going down with Ashley.
We all stood around a fire pit in the front of the house,
in the driveway,
but the smoke kept blowing in our faces
no matter where we stood.

118

Eventually we all went to the backyard,
pounding our drinks,
chain smoking cigarettes,
laughing and fucking around.
Raven's date was a butch girl
in a t-shirt, flat-billed hat and DC shoes.
They were sitting in a chair,
making out
while Ashley, another guy, and I watched,
giggling and laughing.
Eventually
Raven was sitting in the chair
with her pants pulled down partially
while the girl took off the flat-billed hat and gave her pussy a kiss.
Raven busted out laughing,
along with everyone else.
We had been drinking a lot
and somehow Ashley and I ended up
in Sarah's kids' room,
kissing each other hard,
and breathing heavily through our noses.
My hand rested on the back of her head.
She ran her fingers deep and firm
into my greasy hair.
"Oh! Sorry, can I not fuck up your hair?" she asked,
looking sorry.
"I can comb it later."
She pulled me to her,
messing up my hair entirely.
"You're gonna comb it later?"
She kissed me hard and pulled back.
"Yeah."
She kissed me again, breathing in big deep breaths.
"Can I watch you?
It's so fucking sexy when you comb your hair, Danny."
She seemed like such an innocent girl
from a good Mormon family,
but goddamn, that first night she really blew me away.
Right there on the floor.

The beginning of 2008 I spent with Ashley most of the time.
We'd work, close up the diner together, and then go back to the
house—
the empty house—
my father's house.
We'd smoke grass, eat burritos, and have sex
over and over,
again and again.
It was one of those things where
two bodies just fit,
got into a groove together
and took it all the way home
in my green and pink painted bedroom
with a velvet Elvis painting next to London Calling
and Evil Dead posters.
The streetlights had a way of shining in through the blinds
and onto the wooden floor,
giving off this yellow glow—
her naked body covered in yellow and black lines
like a panel from a *Sin City* comic book.

Work was even greater after that.
When we'd run out of ice cream for the milkshakes,
the two of us would go into the freezer together,
neck and get fresh over
oldies playing through the speakers
in the ice cold air.
The nights we spent in each other's arms,
we'd hear these songs
during these beautiful little moments we shared.
And then at work, I'd just go to the jukebox
and play one of 'em.
She'd pass me with plates of food
and give me this look.
I'll never forget it.
She would look at me
like she wanted to just drop those plates,
throw her arms around my neck,
and kiss me.
I knew that look.
While cleaning up at the end of the night,

just the two of us and our manager Carlos,
we'd be refilling the salts, peppers, sugars, and jams,
and gaze at each other from across the diner,
eager to get out and get to each other.
We never offically went out.
I was never her boyfriend
and she was never my girlfriend.
I never knew why.
We had some of the greatest nights together,
the best talks and conversations
which I didn't think was possible with
an eighteen-year-old.
But she was different,
very wise for her age.
Eventually, after a couple months,
I started seeing someone else and so did she.
But even still,
when those opening chords
of "Angel Baby" by Rosie & The Originals
came over the stereo in the diner,
she'd look at me.
And I'd look at her.

Originally we got the band together so I could do an Elvis Presley tribute act. Everyone was always saying how I could make a killing as an Elvis impersonator.

But the day we actually all got together, and once we were all set up, we just started playing Ramones and Cramps songs. We tried playing "That's Alright Mama," but it sounded like The Sex Pistols or something all speed up and manic. When we finished, we looked at each other and laughed our asses off.

On bass, Dick Gonzo, my ex-wife's sassy gay best friend.

On drums, Evelyn or "Bevz" as I called her. She was a fine looking woman and played the drums like an animal.

On guitar, Monty, my best friend and partner in crime. We both felt called by Rock 'n' Roll; we were obsessed with it. It consumed us. So we started practicing, getting down a sets worth and immediately playing out.

None of us could really play our instruments, but began playing shows anyway. We went all out, full throttle. We got buck wild.

Our first show was at the greatest dive bar in town: the P.V. Every friend from every crowd that we hung with was there.

Tables got overturned, glasses broken, beer everywhere with people slipping and falling left and right.

I grabbed ahold of two mic stands like a pair of skis, my feet comically slipping back and forth. It was like a goddamn Benny Hill bit.

That night we only had six songs for our first show. After we played the last one, with the crowd packed shoulder-to-shoulder in this little dive bar, they began begging for more.

We knew a couple covers: "Search & Destroy" by The Stooges and "Human Fly" by The Cramps.

It was like I'd always hoped it'd be—like all those videos I'd seen and studied from the '70s & '80s, where the people in the crowd went apeshit and we expelled every ounce of energy we had, giving it all up to the crowd with them sending it right back.

When we finished the final song I walked outside. The cool March air washed over me. I watched the steam rise off my shoulders and felt my lungs empty the fire inside. It was greater than sex.

After that first show, we never looked back. We kept practicing; our vocals and instruments got tighter and tighter. We booked as many shows as we could, and quickly garnered a reputation around town as that "crazy band" with the singer that takes his clothes off and dances around like a maniac.

We were doing something totally different from anyone in town: a combination of Punk, Rockabilly, and Garage Rock mixed in with frantic, manic, and sloppy Rock 'n' Roll.

So when we'd be playing with the Crust Punks, Grindcore, or whatever, in an industrial area, in a concrete storage space with graffiti covering the walls, they didn't know what to make of us.

Loading in the gear and setting up, I could hear the Punks (in their chains, rags, and spikes on their big boots) talking shit.

"Hey check out fuckin' Elvis. I wonder if they're gonna have a Psychobilly freak out?" They all cracked up. Real tough.

But when we started playing, I saw those same punks after we ripped into that first song. They looked at each other and shrugged and jumped into the growing circle pit.

We gave them no choice but to get their asses moving and shaking. And the shit only got deeper from there.

For as crazy as I could get, my bandmates gave me a run for my money. Dick, Bevz, and Monty all got crazy when drunk.

They'd start fights while I'd stand by, laughing to myself. We were interviewed by *The State Press* one night at the P.V.

It started off with the four of us sitting at the table, drinking beers, answering questions to the red-headed reporter.

By closing time Bevz and Dick were yelling at each other in the parking lot. The acid Monty had taken finally kicked in. He was hanging upside down in a tree, speaking truth as I made out with the reporter by her car.

But that's just the kinda stuff that happened when we hung out; it's what we did.

At Hollywood Alley I got totally naked onstage, tucking my dick back. I was completely out of my head, my eyes bloodshot and raging.

We were asked not to return.

I set up a show at the nursing home I worked at, playing in the summer heat as the seniors chain-smoked cigarettes and didn't budge. Though one lady from the dementia ward danced her ass off.

Playing a packed house at the Yucca Tap Room, we brought it down. The bigger the crowd, the better we played. We fed off energy and in turn gave all we had.

After a set, physically wiped out, with cuts, scrapes, and scratches all over my torso, I had whatever girl I was with take me home early.

Usually, every year during Pride week we'd play shows for the roller derby girls at Ginger's house; everyone in the band dressed in drag. I'd lay on the ground, my hand between my legs and under my dress really cuttin' loose.

We were a fun band and it was a party wherever we were.

After working whatever shit job I had all week long, I'd wait to play again—I quickly became addicted to it all, getting all that energy out, feeling like one of the gods with that microphone, looking over at my best friend while he nailed a staggering solo with that crooked smirk he got when he was in his zone.

It gave us both something that most people never get—something the richest men in the world or kings and queens will never have.

Like Howlin' Wolf said, "And they don't even know about it."
It was something I never knew existed. That feeling when you're singing everything you've got, those bursts of words pumping out from your gut, it's like a shotgun. You're completely surrounded by a crowd of people, yet at the same time you're totally alone in a place where money, class, and all the rest of it no longer matters.

Fuck. They don't even exist.

You can get there if you don't try, if you let yourself get lost in it. It's the thing that's been hypnotizing young men and women since 1954: **raw power.**

TAKE OFF YOUR BOOGIE SHOES

They say that when you die
your mind goes somewhere else,
entirely.
To a peaceful, serene, place,
to your most comforting memories
from your life.
And then for those last few minutes
of brain activity,
after your body has died,
your brain just shuffles
through your memories
backwards through the years,
down to
the child, the toddler, the baby, and finally
back to nothing,
to what it was like before you were born.

Beyond a shadow of a doubt,
I know
one of those last comforting memories
will be of her,
this lady I dated a few months.
We had this thing we would do
where we'd sit on the couch
late at night,
right before going to bed.
She'd sit upright on the couch,
and I'd lay down, putting my head in her lap
while sucking on one of those Japanese soda candies
that she usually had on her.
And she'd run her hands through
my greasy, pomade-covered pomp & ducktail.
No one ever touched my hair
like she did.
This lady really got her fingers in there,
she dug 'em in,
not afraid to get 'em greasy

It felt like my brain was being massaged.
All the bullshit problems,
all the money I didn't have,
all the stress,
all of it
disappeared.
Nothing mattered for those few minutes
during those nights
when we did that thing we did.
A lot of the time
I would fall asleep
and she'd always wake me in the same way.
I won't say how.
I'm saving that one just for me—
just for me and that big sleep I'll take someday
drifting off in her lap
while those fingers dig into my greasy sides,
after my boogie shoes
are put away
and it's *lights out.*

THE LEATHERY GREASERS: A WARNING

I keep coming across these guys
on the bus,
walking the streets,
they're just about everywhere
I am.

Sitting across from one of 'em
on the city bus
spooks me down to my core.
They've got slicked back,
greasy hair
that's turning gray and
tanned, furrowed skin from walking in the sun
too much.
Old-style tattoos,
blurry and faded green,
run up and down their arms,
their lovers names no longer legible
in the little banner around
a simple heart tattoo.
I always wonder where
their women went.
Why aren't they on the bus with them?

One day, I'm
sitting across from this guy,
analyzing him.
He takes a good look at me too:
my slicked back, greasy hair, pale skin, and new tattoos.
It's like he's lookin' back,
and I'm lookin' forward
to a future that just might end up
being my own.

I see this man
down & out,
rolling shitty Top Tobacco cigarettes,
pregnant little toothpick smokes

with loose ends that spill tobacco
all over his lap,
on his faded grey-used-to-be-black
rustler jeans, the cheap kind from K-Mart.
I see him
and it terrifies me
to think
that could be me and my future.
It could be me
if I don't get my shit together.
'Cause right now,
today,
as I get ready to pull this sheet
from the typewriter and catch the
2:48 p.m. bus
I'm going nowhere . . .
Fast.

Miss X

My old man had kicked me out again
(God, how many stories start out this way)
and I had nowhere to go.
I'd been dating Lynn for about a month
and she said I could come stay with her
until I found my own place.
Days turned into weeks
and weeks into months
before I had actually found a place of my own
but
the thought of not being around that girl everyday
kept me right where I was.
After a few months we started working at the same place.
We were always broke,
never had money to go out,
so it became a downward spiral of
work
and
then back home
to sit on that couch,
Lynn in the same pajamas as always
—black with red lips and Playboy bunnies.
We tried to make the best of it.
In the beginning we made love constantly,
neither of us could get enough.
We both got to have orgasms,
so not going out wasn't really a big deal.
Then when we got paid
and actually had a little bit of money
to go out,
to do something,
(like see our friends that we rarely saw
even when we had money)
we still stayed at home.
We'd get tofu and rice
from Chopstix Express,
rent a good documentary or one of our shows.

I'd get stoned and she wouldn't,
we would eat our food,
snuggle up to each other—
not wanting to be anywhere else,
just enjoying each other.
We used to hold hands
after walking out our front door
all the way to the car.
We were like children together,
laughing and cackling,
cracking each other up.
That girl was a funny one,
talking like Kenny Powers,
or kicking her legs
in fast, quick, little, kicks.
We'd squeeze each other's faces
because we both had big cheeks—
we looked like chipmunks.
We laughed until we had drool pouring from our mouths,
tears in our eyes, and that pain you get in your throat.
I had never been so in love.
Her parents were rich
and sometimes we'd go to their house
in the desert
when they were out of town.
Getting into their big Jacuzzi bathtub,
we'd make love with Billie Holiday
playing from a radio in the corner,
then smoke cigarettes together
on the back porch,
and just listen to the sounds of the night.
She was a good woman;
she treated me nice.
She didn't yell.
She didn't play bullshit games.
But then, eventually,
like all good things,
something changed.
We stopped holding hands.
We stopped making love.
We stopped laughing like we once had.

We just lost it.
I knew it in my gut.
I asked her if she wanted to end it.
I knew she did,
but she wouldn't say it.
She couldn't be the one to call it off.
So I did.
Right there in Pet Smart.
For some reason,
women,
the ones I've dealt with . . .
they can never say it.
They always leave it up to me,
and they shouldn't do that—
Because I love change.

The Inbred Aristocats

We were sitting outside like we sometimes do in the evenings, when we're sick of staring at a screen. My gal is a real cat woman. We have neighbors that feed the stray cats in the apartment complex. Whole families of different cats. Throughout the day, they'd sprawl about in shaded spots of grass, and move with the sun.

Rachael would walk up to a few of them lounging there in the grass. She'd crouch down in her little kimono and scratch them, and pet them, and smile and laugh with them.

She always did this. One time, however, she stood back up and walked back towards me, picking up rocks along the way. I'd been leaning against the little fence on our tiny porch, having a smoke or two, and watching her. She started throwing those rocks at the lounging cats. I couldn't stop laughing.

"What?" she asked.

"Nothin."

"I think these cats are inbred."

"Oh yeah? How can you tell?"

"See that orange cat?" she pointed.

"Yeah."

"Look at his head. His eyes are all big, they take up his whole head almost."

Then the cats walked by in a single line. Like the fuckin' aristocats or something. An inbred Disney flick, come to life.

"Here he comes, look!"

And she was right. All the cats were hesitant to cross in front of us on the porch. At the very end of the line of cats was a little kitten. It was the most hesitant of all. Rachael walked right up to it, wanting to play with that little kitten.

"Hey, don't do that. You're gonna separate it from the group," I hollared.

The kitten ran off in the other direction, away from the others in line, and far out of sight.

"Motherfucker," she grumbled.

The line of cats had rushed past us and were gone.

"Well I hope he find his way back to them," she said, with a sigh.

Four more cats came and spread out in the grass. A completely different family of cats. They began to bathe each other, lick behind each others' ears when the sprinklers came on and Rachael laughed loudly.

"Hahahahaha! They scattered like roaches!"

We stood close to each other, my hand around her waist pulling her in tight. Laughin' and akissin'.

The outdoor lights in the apartment complex flickered on as the sun set in the west.

"You hungry?"

"Yeah. Breakfast for dinner?"

"You got it baby. Blueberry or buttermilk?"

"Pssh. That's easy, blueberry."

MY PLACE

We're in many different places.
For some
it's a basement
or a motel room.
For others
it's a kitchen table
with all the lights off,
just the single bulb ahead.

We spend our nights
smoking and typing,
sharpening our senses
with drink or smoke
and typing for hours,
night after night.
Klick klick klick ding shhhhhhhht . . .

For me, it always comes back to the porch.
Everywhere I move
I always end up on the porch.
Never without the
Kerr "Self-Sealing" wide mouth Mason jar,
full of ice cold water
constantly refilled throughout the night,
always dripping with condensation
even at night.
It's fuckin' burnin' up outside.
Ya gotta suffer for it
though.
That's what makes the difference.

Right now
someone is alone in a room
pacing back and forth
burning themselves with a cigarette,
staring at a page.
They're the only ones that

will ever see it.
Either the drink or the drug
will take them first.
Or they just slip into and get lost in
the madness.
Then they become as
indecipherable
as the academic intellectuals.

Hell,
it could happen to me too.
We'll see what happens.
Keeping it going
every night,
standing on the porch
pouring it out,
sending off a weekly
5 poems,
getting it out there
like so many do.
We're in many different places.

Flat broke.
Eleven bucks to my name.
But I didn't care,
I was gonna get a pack of smokes
and a burrito anyways.
A guy's gotta live sometime.

Walking past the dirt lot
behind the gas station,
I spotted a ten-dollar bill
smiling up at me from the dirt and rocks.
I snatched it up
and ran with it held up in the air.
"Woooo hoooo!" I hollered,
running and skipping
all the way to Losbetos.

Walking back,
a bean & cheese in my hand,
smokes rolled up in my shirt sleeve
and a shit-eating grin on my face,
I passed the dirt lot again.
There was a guy with his head down,
scrounging for something in the dirt.
"Ya lose something?" I asked.
"Yeah . . . thirty fuckin' bucks, man.
A ten and a twenty."
"Shit, that sucks," I said, feeling a bit bad.
"Can I get a cigarette?" he asked,
pointing to the rolled up pack in my sleeve.
"Sure," I said, pulling a Pall Mall
and handing it to him.
"Thanks."
"Don't mention it."
I don't normally bum smokes
to people I don't know.
But

I had to.
I mean, he paid for 'em.
Now, every time I walk by that dirt lot,
I find myself scanning the ground
looking for that missing twenty.
Every time.

OCCUPY AN AK-47

This Sunday morning
before work
I'm standing outside,
typing this,
as crows and pigeons
peck at a McDonald's bag
laying in a handicap parking space.
The country is on fire right now.
Protests and demonstrations are spreading
across the country.
They're calling it
the "Occupy" movement.
It started in NYC
with people occupying shit,
taking up space,
camping in the streets,
demanding change,
and a release
from the banks' stranglehold
on the country.
But it's all in vain.

After a few days they
send in the riot squad
with their shields and big sticks.
Dozens are maced and arrested in Boston.
This makes me really sad
because it's so fucking great
that people
have finally had enough,
that they're out there
trying something.
But what they don't realize
is that
this isn't the sixties.
A simple "sit-in"
won't release the corporations'

grip from around our throats.
Are you fucking kidding me?
There's far too much money involved.
Billions.
A lot of the people,
the young ones especially,
think it'll all work.
The banks will finally break down
and just give in.
But they won't.
There's money to be made
and ten thousand camping protesters
won't put a stop to it.

They sleep in tents,
and have drum circles,
and sit in lawn chairs,
and play on their iPad's,
and kick around a hacky sack,
and smoke weed and fuck in the parks.
And they can't agree on
just what they want.
They have no representative.
There's no face to the movement,
because no one seems to
have the slightest idea
just what the fuck they're after.
Camping in the streets hundreds of feet
below the high-rise buildings of the rich elite
has (thus far) not done one thing,
and it's no wonder.
It takes money in the bank,
blood in the streets,
to topple an empire.
We've become a country of
pussies and crybabies,
afraid to throw a brick
or a Molotov cocktail,
too scared to take it to the
monsters that keep us

locked up and held down.
(Except for those bad asses in Oakland who wouldn't stand down.)

Nope, it's all about
peace, love, and equality,
man.
Which are all
good things,
great things.
But when you're dealing with
the demons of Wall Street
it's going to take more than a peacful
sit-in
to bring them down
and take our country back.
Can't they see that?

Isn't it obvious by now?
The working class has little to no say
in this new movement.
It's easy for the
young college kids
with trust funds to live off of
while they camp out in protest
and "take their stand."
But what about us?
Those of us with minimum wage jobs
and food stamps.
We can't go camp out
day & night.
We've got kids to feed,
rents to pay,
lights to keep on,
jobs to show up at.
Where is our say, our voice?

I don't know what the right answer is,
what the way is,
but I do know it's not this.
You'll see.
Time will tell you.
But are people really ready?

Ready to die for it,
to bleed for it
and, if need be,
to kill for it?
When the real revolution comes,
when the
construction workers, telemarketers, deli clerks,
teachers, fast food workers, bus drivers,
pizza delivery guys, day laborers,
baggage handlers, pimps, drug dealers, and cashiers—
when Americans really begin the fight,
when they take it to the streets
with a plan,
with gritted teeth & clenched fists,
I will be there
with my son by my side
and the firm belief
"Give me peace, or I will show you Death."

My mother has this dog. It looks like a wolf, but apparently she's a Malamute.

Her name is Lacey and never has a name fit so well. She's the most lady-like dog I've ever seen. The way she moves and sits with such grace and sophistication.

She's snow white, with black/grey on top and a little half-mask around her eyes. It's like black eyeliner. Her eyelashes are long & curve upward.

She's kind of a lazy dog. She'll just lie around all day, dozing and sighing out breaths of air. But the first opportunity she gets, she'll bolt on you. Run away like the wind. In a matter of seconds, she's a blur on the horizon. Then she'll slow down, stop, even let you get real close to her and then take off again in five or six easy strides.

My mom loves that fuckin' dog. Buys her expensive dog food and doggy chocolate chip cookies. She takes her everywhere with her—doctor's appointments, social gatherings. All the neighborhood kids are always coming by to see "the wolf."

My mom just moved into a new apartment in a quiet area; it's more like a duplex. There's a little backyard with grass growing. And now Lacey begs me to let her out when I go outside to type at night. She doesn't sniff around or play in the grass. No. She sits at my feet and sleeps with the crickets chirping loudly and the night birds, one or two, singing & talking. Lacey sleeps the most peaceful sleep out there. It can't all be box fans and a/c units. No, the wolf needs to be amongst its prey. So it can sleep the good sleep—the sleep of lions, bears, and tigers. The sleep of the confident killer.

Sleep without fear.

Part Five

Two Smokes and the Summer Rain

Used to smoke a pack a day,
now it's just two cigarettes
at evening time,
when the lady is in the shower
and after the reefer
has been smoked.
I sit on the ledge of our patio,
legs stretched out,
exhaling long trails of smoke,
observing
the busy apartment complex,
mainly blacks & Mexicans
with a dash of Apache Junction
white trash.

Two girls
in their early twenties
sit on a bench in the little courtyard
talking loudly,
gesturing wildly
about some bitch neither can stand.
Purple lightning flashes overhead,
illuminating the courtyard.
Then it begins to sprinkle.
And then it starts to rain.

A woman walks down the stairs from her apartment.
She's barefoot and smiling,
head tilted up towards the sky,
taking in deep breaths
of the good smell of rain.
I imagine she's been waiting for this.
Waiting on the rain.
In her apartment.
It's really started coming down.
She couldn't light her cigarette,
the rain was dropping from everywhere.

Two children
run and skip down the sidewalk
with their mother running close behind.
Her arms, both of them,
full of mail, grocery bags, and a baby.
"Hurry, hurry, hurry up. C'mon, the mail is getting wet
and I got Netflix here, goddamnit, move your asses."

A man in a motorized wheelchair
emerges from one of the halls
across the courtyard.
I watch his electric chair
buzz by on the sidewalk.
He was going for a full lap
of the place it seemed.
When he passed me, I saw
droplets of rain
breaking on his face and streaming down.
Grinning ear to ear,
he winked one eye at me,
made me smile.

This is Arizona.
Rain in the summer is a gift.
Means a lot to us. All of us.

Date Night Surprise

We really couldn't afford it, but I got the tickets anyway. We hadn't been out of the apartment for months. Didn't have the money to go do anything. Ever.

Louis C.K. was our favorite comedian, so I figured, even if we had to live off grilled cheese for the next week, it'd be worth it. To be able to forget everything—the bills, the jobs, the bullshit stress—to escape that for a couple hours and just laugh our asses off would do us a world of good.

I kept it a secret, wanting to surprise my lady, and give her a well-deserved thrill. I told her we were going to downtown Phoenix to get a drink at a 1920s themed bar.

On the freeway, just after sundown, we were headed to the theater, guided by the GPS. We both were having full-blown panic attacks as the cars and trucks whizzed by us at over 80 mph, all bumper to bumper. We missed our exit. The GPS redirected us and we pulled off at the next exit. But just when she went to turn, I saw the one-way street sign and a car coming right at us.

"SHIT! No, no, don't! This is a one-way street," I yelled. She jerked the wheel back and we continued straight.

The machine kept talking, "Up at Jefferson . . . make a left turn." But it was another one-way street. I threw the thing down on the floor, after shutting it off.

"Why'd you do that?"

"That piece of shit is getting us lost. We're only a block away. Just park it there," I told her, pointing to the side.

We parked on a deserted, dark, lonely street and walked the block to the theater. As we approached the front, with the big sign that spelled out: "Louis C.K." in big yellow letters, my lady started asking questions.

"So, what are we doing? Just getting a drink and going home? I don't think I can drink if I gotta drive home on that hectic freeway. *Ugh.* Is it too much to ask to just have FUN? Just this one night?"

"No, darlin'. It's not. That's why I . . . got tickets," I said, standing under the marquee with a big, shit-eating grin on my face.

For a moment, it didn't quite register with her.

"Wha-what? Seriously?! Are you fucking with me? You better not be joking," she said.

"No honey. It's no joke. I mean, they're just balcony/nose bleed seats--" with people walking & rushing around us. She pulled me in close and smiled up at me with that million-dollar smile. She kissed me, pulling me in tight and grabbed my ass. Our tongues danced in our mouths.

"Baby, you really know how to make a gal feel special. First, roses this morning and now you surprise me with tickets to Louis? I love you so fucking much, Danny."

Inside, we sat with the other poor folks, packs of middle-aged couples, groups of teenage boys and geeks in Star Wars t-shirts. It was a great night. Strangers struck up conversations with one another, all laughing and sharing their favorite Louis C.K. bits.

Finally the comedian took the stage. After a roaring, packed-house, standing ovation, everyone quieted down and for the next two hours we didn't have any bills, rent, electricity payments, jobs, bullshit. Just laughs to be had. And it was so great, like gospel. Everything we thought in our heads, everything the two of us talked about at home, everything that made us crazy with anger, he was up there talking about—reaffirming what we already knew to be true—dumb parents who didn't discipline their kids properly, or how, when you try to delete your Facebook, it sends numerous pop-ups trying to get you to log back in and stay connected. That night the comedian helped us forget our troubles and laugh at the bullshit society continues to eat up.

Comedians, poets, musicians . . . these artists should really be called therapists. Those two hours of sitting & laughing did so much for us. By the time we walked back to the car on that deserted, dark, lonely street, we felt better. Standing by the car, I put my hands on the waist of her dress and pulled her close to me.

"So, were you surprised? Did I show you a good time, Mama?"

"Danny that was the sweetest thing. Thank you for making it a surprise. You really got me."

And we kissed in front of an old school house with its huge white pillars and yellow light overhead. A cold wind blew.

"I'm glad you had a good time darlin'. Now let's get in the car and get outta here."

We really couldn't afford it, but it was okay.

The rent could wait another week.

Lowlife Urbanity

Let me tell ya, that apartment complex we lived in—it was something else. A mini-ghetto in the middle of suburbia, before you reached the Mormon mansions of Mesa. I saw and heard everything that went on there with so many characters living out their lives.

We had The Natty Ice Walrus. He parked his truck in front of the office and he always had a beer in his left hand. A Natural Ice. Might as well have been glued to his hand. I never saw him without it. I'd see him driving around in his truck slurping that beer, licking his white walrus-like moustache. He'd open his mailbox with his red leather skin and perma-frown and shuffle along in flip-flops.

Then there was the skinny, tattooed lady that asked me for muscle relaxers in the laundry room. She was married to a hulk of a man. I'd always see his big, bald, tattooed head. He looked like Bam Bam Bigelow. The two would walk along with their little girl in tow. One night, I saw the skinny tattooed lady walking away from her place with a little, skinny guy. She wore a hoodie up over her head, and constantly looked over her shoulder as they walked on by. Now I see her all the time with different men that aren't her husband. He must not have enough Somas to keep her at home.

And, of course, there was the pot-bellied convict with the "white pride" tattoo across his back. He gave me a joint once, asked me if I wanted to smoke some meth. I declined, graciously.

Then there was my neighbor. Middle-aged, tan, with a gold earring on the left side. I was on the porch one night, listening to The Velvet Underground. He came outside and asked if I could turn it up.

"I'm a Lou Reed fan from back in the day. Turn that shit up, kid!" he said, with a wink of his eye.

He ordered the same two escorts on a weekly basis. One chubby white girl and one long-legged black lady. They never said hi to me or anything, just walked on by in their clear high heels.

It's amazing what one could see and hear from that porch of mine.

One cold, December night, my buddy, T-Bird, and I were on the porch, chain-smoking and jamming on some Little Richard when, from the parking lot, we could hear voices arguing. From my porch I saw the muzzle flash, followed by the deafening sound of gunshots. POP. POP. POP. POP. It echoed loudly throughout the complex. Instinctively, I hit the ground while my friend just stood there. We rushed inside and shut the door. From outside we heard yelling. Spanish. Then came the screams. I reached over and unplugged the Christmas tree, just as I had seen my parents do when I was a boy and gunshots would ring out from somewhere in the neighborhood. Lying on my belly, listening intently, came the sound of two cars starting up and peeling out.

But still, nighttime in the complex is the best time.

I can sit in the dark on the porch and contentedly listen to the sounds of the night in my suburban ghetto. The poorest part of town.

Couples fighting and screaming about money. Glass crashing and shattering. Loud thuds against the walls, children crying.

Parents terrorizing their kids for wetting the bed. "Look at it!" they'd scream, over and over again, getting louder and louder.

I'd watch the worst amateur drug dealer in the world and the never-ending traffic at his apartment. Someone gets out of a car and runs inside. A minute later, they run back out. When they open their car door, I hear someone shout from inside "Did ya get it? Did ya get it?"

Then tonight, while I stood outside typing this, the skinny tattooed lady was out walking around—rather, stumbling around—with the tan bachelor from next door. I could hear them talking on his porch. So I walked over as it began to rain and the thunder rumbled. I asked if he had a smoke.

"They're homemade," he said.

"Shit, that's the best kind." I took one and thanked him.

The skinny tattooed lady stood, leaned against the door, doing the "nod," struggling to keep her eyes open.

"So you got the whole seventies hairstyle going, huh?"

"Eh, more of a 1920's style."

The tan bachelor nodded his head, smiling big, chuckling to himself.

"Alright, lady. Let's get you home."

The rain was starting to come down now, sprinkling hard.

"You guys take it easy. Thanks again for the smoke. I appreciate it," I told them, as they walked off together towards the apartment she shared with her husband. I watched him put his hand on her waist as she stumbled and fell on her ass. He put out his hand to her and she took it as he hoisted her back on her feet. He looked back at me and smiled like the Devil.

That apartment complex was something else.

Let me tell ya.

The Lady at the End

My apartment complex is spread out in clusters of six apartments, connected by one walkway. At the opposite end from me, lives a prostitute. She has a little girl—three or four years old. They're constantly walking past me. The little girl is always smiling and saying "Hello," and giving a childlike wave. Sometimes the lady is impatient with her, jerking her arm and yelling, "COME ON, TANNER." Then other times—most of the time—she's sweet and speaks softly and gently to her little girl.

I'm unemployed and here at the apartment most of the day and so is she. She walks past me on the porch, waddling by in a miniskirt so short that the bottom cheeks of her fat ass bounce and jiggle in waves. Free as a bird. And, of course, she's got massive fat tits that she flaunts in shirts that don't fit. She just jiggles all over the place: ass, legs, tits.

Different men visit her on a weekly basis:

—the Asian guy in the European sportscar.

—the metrosexual Mexican guy, in the Affliction shirt and square shoes.

—the two big black guys in Roca Wear.

—the middle-aged white guy, with a holster for his iPhone.

Last night, she went out with a blonde & orange girlfriend of hers. She looked like a dancer, a stripper. They were walking by and her friend's clear high heels were really loud on the concrete walkway and she said, "Ugh. I feel like a hooker." I couldn't contain myself. I cackled with laughter while standing at my typewriter with a Mason jar of water and a pack of Pall Malls.

"Don't! It's not funny!" she whined at me.

"No, it's pretty funny actually."

"In a good way or a bad way?"

"Take your pick, lady."

"Elvis! That wasn't very nice . . ." the lady at the end said.

"Oh. Well, you two enjoy your Friday night."

"Okay, you too! . . . wait . . . is it Friday? No. It's Saturday . . . HEY ELVIS!" she shouted, "IT'S SATURDAY, NOT FRIDAY!"

"See? Shows what I know."

Just as they started up the girlfriend's big truck and the subwoofer started to boom, a guy pulled up and got out of his car. The lady from the end told her friend something and got out of the truck. She walked up to him, rubbing his chest, and he took a look around, seeing me, turned his head and fixed his gaze to the far end of the walkway. She walked him down to the very end of the walkway and she let him inside her place. They came back before I could even finish my cigarette. I'm pretty sure the lady knew that I knew what she did for a living, because every time I'd see her after that she had this look in her eyes,

Like,

Yeah?

So what?

THE DEATH PARTY OF MY DREAMS

We were having a dinner party,
my girlfriend and I.
All of the guests
were dead people.
Famous ones like
John Dillinger
Elvis Presley
Jim Morrison
Billy the Kid
Frida Kahlo
Charles Bukowski.
Rachael and I sat at a large table,
that we didn't have,
drinking, smoking reefer, and laughing away
while Billy the Kid & Dillinger played a game of cards.
Elvis whispered in Freida's ear, while she bit her lip.
Bukowski and Morrison shared a bottle of wine
in the corner, talking low.

Rachael answered a sudden knock at the door,
and there she was.
The Black Dahlia herself,
Elizabeth Short.
Looking sexy, healthy, and in one piece.
My girlfriend showed her around,
introduced her to everyone.
Bukowski was hypnotized,
he hadn't seen a woman like this in decades.
My girlfriend noticed him staring and she said,
"Hank, you just behave yourself!
Miss Short is doing some shots with me . . ."
Rachael took her to the kitchen and they downed a few,
the two of them laughing and giggling,
talking about their hair and their clothes.
Then Elizabeth asked to use the restroom.
She went down the hall and stopped just outside the door
to stare at a series of pictures on the wall.

Rachael was obsessed with the Dahlia murder
and had four framed pictures
of the crime scene
on the wall.
Elizabeth's little body cut in half,
her face sliced up into a grin,
cut at the sides of her mouth.

The entire party stopped
playing cards
flirting
drinking
whispering
and everyone just watched.
Elizabeth's body began to shake,
her knees buckled slightly
in her high heels.
She let out this sound,
this scream.
Some covered their ears it was so loud.
She ripped the pictures from the wall,
stomping them,
breaking the glass in the frames.
Then she fell to the floor,
frantically tearing the pictures from the frames,
the glass shards stabbing into her little hands,
but she didn't even notice.
She just kept tearing,
ripping
until the pictures were in shreds.
Rachael tried to help her up
but caught a punch to the head.
Elizabeth yelled at her,
"IT WASN'T SUPPOSED TO BE THIS WAY!
I WAS GONNA BE A STAR!!!"
She ran for the door,
but Bukowski blocked her exit.
A drink in his hand, a cigarette in his mouth
he slowly spoke,
"Baby . . . I know it's a lot to take at once. But listen . . ."
"GET OUT OF MY WAY, YOU AWFUL MAN!"

"LISTEN . . . you did become a star.
Your name was in the papers for years.
It was the greatest unsolved murder in L.A. history.
You are a star. They made movies about you baby . . ."
Elizabeth wiped the black, running mascara from her face.
"They did?"
"Yes. Come here . . ."
Hank took her to the corner of the room,
Morrison helped wipe away her tears, brushed her hair gently, and
picked the glass from her hands
saying,
"It's alright baby . . . it's cool . . ."
Then Elvis sang a song,
Freida whipped up a painting real quick,
Billy & Dillinger shot up the place with pistols,
and then I woke up.

To the Lost

It was a suicide.
He had gotten drunk,
too drunk.
Tried going to the bar he worked at,
it was his night off,
but they turned him away.
"You've already had too much to drink.
Go sleep it off, pal."
Instead he went home,
put a glock to his head
and blew his brains out
on his back porch.
His roommate found him.
There was no note.
There were no answers,
just questions left behind.

A week later was the memorial service.
He was an atheist,
a vocal one at that.
Had a tattoo of a rotting zombie Christ
on his arm.
But his family were devout Lutherans,
so that was the send-off he got.

Standing against the wall,
in the small chapel,
I saw the lines were clearly divided.
Seated in the pews were people
dressed in calm, muted colors.
Pastels.
Blues, greens, pinks, yellows, and lavenders.
Those were his blood relatives
and Lutheran members of the family's church.

Then on the edges and in the back
stood and sat his other family:
the metal heads, the punks, the hardcore kids.

The subculture misfits.
Dressed in black,
arms & legs tattoed with ink.

The pastels
spoke in unison, reciting prayers and scripture,
while the kids in black, stood silent,
unmoved by the minister's words about Christ.
The pastels bowed their heads in prayer for the poor boy's soul.
We, in black, looked around the room,
studying their pinched faces.
One woman apparently could feel my stare,
'cause she opened her eyes, and looked right into mine.
Never will forget that look,
like she knew something I didn't.

The minister in the white and green robe kept talking,
saying my friend was in the loving arms of Jesus.
Guess he forgot that suicides got
a one-way ticket straight to hell.
It was typical.
A spiritual buffet,
take what you like,
ignore what you don't.
But I don't blame them, not one bit.
What parent wants to imagine
their child burning in that lake of fire,
never to be held in their arms again?
No one.

His mother went up and said a few words,
some stories,
funny ones from his childhood.
His neighbor stood up and spoke,
then an old girlfriend from high school.
And then a great silence.
The podium stood empty.
Before I knew it,
my hands were gripping the wooden podium
and my mouth was talking,
telling the pastels & black shirts
about the first time I saw him.

158

He was in the mosh pit doing spin kicks and backflips
like a five-foot-six, blonde ninja in Saucony jazz shoes.
And how I never saw him be unkind or mean to anyone,
that he was a GOOD boy.
My eyes began to burn,
I felt my throat tightening.
"Really gonna miss him," I managed to choke out.
I took my place back against the wall
as the slideshow & music started up.
They were playing The Beatles.
My friend was a Black Sabbath kind of guy.

Outside I saw faces not seen in years,
not since I was a 17-year-old kid.
I saw Matty, my friend, standing alone.
We had just buried another one
of the boys from the crew,
Munster,
less that six months earlier.
Matty and I were the only ones left.
Went straight up to him,
sobbing & shaking, we both latched on,
hugging each other as tight as we could.
"It's too much, man. It's too soon. They're both fucking GONE."
Matty was broken and I was worried about him.
Very much so.

Then we all met at a bar,
his bar,
the one he worked at
and got turned away from that night.
We told stories
like when everyone was trying to fuck this girl
and he wasn't,
but she pulled him into a room
at the end of the night . . .
picking *him* over us all.
Or how he could make his balls do all kinds of tricks,
disappearing and reappearing in his red nutsack.
"The popper" he called it.

We slammed down shots & brews,
burying our little buddy, one glass at a time.

And the last thing . . .
His parents showed up at the bar,
cradling T-shirts on hangers, his clothes.
I saw someone pick up his Blood For Blood shirt.
It had been OUR shirt, we shared it back and forth.
We both loved that band.
They sang about "living in exile" like we both did.
"Shit, that was our shirt," I said to the table of drunks
and grieving friends.
"Well, go get it, man. Go on."
I went up to the guy holding it.
"Hey man, that shirt means a lot to me, can I . . ."
Before I could finish, it was in my hands.
The guy gave a generous smile,
"Then you should have it."
I sat back down at the table of friends,
holding the shirt up to my face.
He lingered in my nose, one last time.
But my little buddy was gone,
a faded T-shirt, his scent and a few funny stories
were all that remained.
We all toasted one last shot.
I said,
    "to the lost . . ."
and the table of old friends all repeated,
    "To the lost."
Rest well in your dreamless sleep, pal.
Down the hatch.
Watch it go
with a Black Tooth Grin.

THE GOOD GUY

Just lost another job—
the good one,
the one I was supposed to keep awhile.
So now
my lady and I
are living at my mom's.
After staying at my dad's for only a week,
he kicked us out
because the floors weren't mopped.
I had been gone job hunting
all day
and was planning on doing the floors that night.
He wasn't due home until the next day.
But he came home early
and was furious.
He stomped around the house
with the mop,
cleaning the floors,
snarling in my face,
"You're a no-good, punk bitch, always fuckin' have been . . ."

We moved into my mother's little apartment
that same day.
That was yesterday.

Tonight
I pulled an upside down plastic laundry hamper
in between my legs.
Seated on a red & white ice chest,
I set my typewriter up.
It's all I can do tonight.
When things continuously
go wrong
and then constantly
get worse
for days, weeks, months, even years at a time,
when you're down

and you can't get up
and they're just kicking you
over and over
and just outside the circle of kicking legs
you can see a little boy
watching you get beaten
while the elders just shake their heads and say,
"I don't know what to tell ya.
Don't know what to tell ya' . . ."
I guess
I just gotta
get up
stay up
and throw those hard punches.

But You'll Never Follow Me

I got home
from my buddy's house;
they had a cookout.
My girlfriend was supposed to come
with,
but
she stayed home instead.

I come home and
am kissing on her,
admiring her in a new vintage dress.
I ask to use her phone
to call my mom
for a ride to my job interview.
The call log came up
and I saw a man's name
I had never seen in her phone
before tonight.
I asked her who it was,
and she grew silent for
a second.
Just long enough to
let me know
what was up.
"Who is it?"
She still didn't answer.
"Who is it?!"
I got louder,
my fists were clenched,
my teeth grinding,
the vein in my head
throbbing.
"It's a guy."
Then we got into it . . .
"From where?"
"A website . . ."
I picked up the laptop

and set it in her lap.
"Show him to me," I said,
my whole body shaking.
It felt like I was gonna
throw up.
He was a trust-fund kid
from New York City
that was into
everything
"vintage."
It made perfect sense.
I thought back to all the things she said,
all the promises
and words of love.
Jesus Christ.
What did I expect?
We'd been together a year and a half.
I'd had over six jobs
in that time period.
Something always went wrong,
out of my hands—
hours got cut in my department,
company went out of business,
lay-offs . . .
always something.
I keep trying,
keep at it,
looking for that great job
that'll make it all okay.
But it's too late.
We're living in my father's house,
sleeping on a small,
stiff-as-wood,
full-sized bed.
She never sleeps.
We don't go out.
We hardly have sex anymore.
We never have energy
for anything
besides watching TV

or
cooking dinner.
Not to mention
my
psycho ex-wife,
kid,
no car/no driver's license.
What did I expect?
It's the suburban rut,
the American nightmare,
and now she's running scared.

We sat and talked
for nearly two hours.
Her explaining
how lonely she is
and how it's not entirely her fault.
She says I can't
take care of her,
I'm not a man.
She was
supposed to be the one
that fit with me,
that saw it through
to the very end.
Now she's in the bedroom
and I'm on the couch.
I've never had this before,
where the thought of
sleeping alone
is terrifying.
Not exciting,
like it used to be
when I was desperate to
get out of a relationship.
Nope.
I'm losing the big one.
The only one I ever had eyes for.
I just can't get it right.

I can never seem to warm up
these days.
It's freezing all day,
my feet like popsicles,
pale, white, and frozen.
Winter is really
hitting Arizona.
It's
wet
gray
painful.
Ian Curtis and Hank Williams
weep into the black clouds above.

Walking to the bus stop
my freshly shaved bald head
numb from the cold.
The pomp—
the greasy combed hair—
gone
since my pin-up girlfriend,
the Marilyn to my Elvis,
packed up and left,
the week before Christmas.
I can't say I really blame her,
I can't say she didn't try.
She stuck it out a good while.
She left because I can't hold down
a job
and because
I caught her going behind my back
with another man
that combed his hair too.
Secret conversations
with a guy that had what I didn't—
vintage wool suits,
an apartment in New York City,

and exotic antiques.
No matter how handsome a bum, though,
eventually
he doesn't stand a chance.
She used to joke about it even,
"Ya know, you're lucky you're so handsome."
I forgot to tell her,
good looks only get you so far
and they don't last very long.

But I got a job.
Actually,
started it the day she left for Tucson.
It's a place that represents small business office suppliers of
paper, ink toner, pens, pencils.
They get small offices to ditch the corporate
staples office max kinkos office depot
and go with small business suppliers instead.
Stimulate the local economy they say.
It's a cool gig,
pays high commissions and is a real quiet place.

It sits in a business district that's right next to
an artificial lake,
a big winding one,
going around medium-sized lakeside houses
with tiny docks and tiny boats.
It's so close.
It's just right there
out the back door,
next to the radio blaring AC/DC.
Outside it's like an entire other world.
Not Arizona.
Green waters,
thick green grass,
little green shits
from the green-headed
mallard ducks.
There're pairings of them all over;
a lady said they mate for life.
Those mallards,

they give all that fake stuff life,
they make it real.
On our smoke breaks we all go out there,
most everybody just stands
and smokes on a little back porch area,
laughing, joking, telling stories,
putting the cigarette butts neatly in a coffee can.

Sometimes I'll walk away from the group
and stand at the green/blue water's edge
and stare at the concrete shelf of the fake lake
just beneath the water—
the real dirt
concealed beneath the murky blue/green mixture—
And everyday
I miss her
a little bit
less
and a little bit
less
with every
fake wave
that rolls in.
I just gotta warm up.
Winter has really hit Arizona.

"But darlin', how are we gonna get back home tonight? The buses don't run after ten o'clock and I don't have a dollar to my name," I said, fastening the clip to my tie. The third button from the top.

"Baby, come on. I have over two-hundred dollars left. I'll pay for us to get a cab home. Get on the web and check to see how much it'll be," she said, applying her makeup.

"Okay, hold on."

She had three days left on her trip.

If things went well, she'd be moving back here so we could date.

That afternoon she heard me arguing with my ex-wife on the phone and she'd been acting real strange ever since. Distant and detached.

She didn't gaze at me with that look she had when I picked her up from the airport.

No, something was off now.

I could feel it.

However, I never expected what was about to happen that night.

Never.

But I should've.

I mean, a girl with the nickname "Crazy Michele" should've been warning enough, but you see I'm stupid and I tend to believe people.

"It's only 44 bucks!" I called to the bathroom.

"Awesome. It's cheaper than getting a hotel for the night," she said, slinking back into the room in a vintage, tight black dress.

"So you ready to go Doggie Daddy?"

"Let's go, Mama."

We went to an oyster house called Casey Moore's where my dead friend used to work.

We took a walk of the outside patio area, carrying our drinks, looking for a place to sit.

There was none.

Luckily, within two minutes, a big group got up to leave.

"It's so weird. I don't recognize ANYONE here. Do you?"

"No . . ." she said, her stare bouncing from one person to the other.

I could feel her growing anxious, not knowing anyone, not having anyone's attention, except mine.

She slurped down a plate of oysters and made me try a couple. I didn't like 'em.

We barely got through two drinks when she was wanting to leave, wanting to go to the best dive bar in Tempe—the P.V.—the Palo Verde Lounge, a hangout for scumbags & assholes, right where we belonged.

We hoofed it over there a few miles, through the backstreets of the neighborhood.

We get there and it's dead. Ten people there, maybe a couple of old friends from way back, drinking buddies, no one real close.

She got us some drinks and I took over the jukebox.

We both chatted with the few people we knew: this creeper dude with his arm around Michele's waist talking about how in love with her he was, and then later a guy with long, blonde hair by the jukebox.

She grabbed me and pulled me over by the pool tables.

We danced and she grinded herself into me as The Stooges played.

But it was all over when she spotted this guy in hipster Buddy Holly glasses. I couldn't get a word in and she acted like I wasn't there.

So I pulled up a stool and sat back at the bar sipping my beer while she and that guy played pool.

Ten minutes later I come back from the bathroom and they're gone.

"No fuckin' way," I said under my breath.

I walked outside and checked the side of the building and was actually shocked NOT to find her making out with that guy.

I circled the whole building.

They were long gone.

I went back inside.

"Hey did anyone see where Michele went?"

"Yeah, she took off with that guy with the glasses . . ." the bartender said.

"Mother . . . fucker."

I sent a text.

"Did you really just leave with that other guy?"

Twenty minutes later I got a reply:

"Yeah. I'm just goin' with the flow. The night is young. You are gorgeous . . . I am sure you will figure a way. If all else fails, kiss some bitch, fuck her, and send me a video of it."

The only thing that made any sense to say was "WHAT THE FUCK?!"

Seriously?

Not a cent to my name or in my wallet. I could've just walked back in the bar, announced my troubles to the few friends I had and gotten a ride home, but no, I'm stubborn and, like I said, stupid, so I just started walking east.

Twenty miles and four hours later and I was back at my father's house unlacing my shoes and getting ready to pop the blisters when my old man walks by the open door to my room.

"Did you just get home?"

"Yeah."

"Where's Michele?"

"That cunt left me at the bar last night. Just took off with some other guy. Dad . . . I'm so fuckin mad . . . I could kill her. It was a really long walk."

"Are you fuckin' kidding me? Seriously?"

"Yup."

"Why didn't you call me? I'd of gotten up and picked up your ass."

"It was like two a.m. I didn't think you'd hear the phone."

"No, I would've gotten you."

"My phone actually died like ten minutes after I started walking. I went by Monty's apartment, thinking I could just crash there, but he wasn't home."

"What the fuck, son? Jesus christ, I'm sorry. That's fucked up. You don't just leave somebody like that. Goddamnit. Still just a crazy fuckin' bitch, huh? Is that her shit right there?" He pointed to the open suitcase with all her shit piled around it.

"Yeah."

"Well what the fuck's it still doin' in the house?"

We both broke into the same wide devilish grins.

"Throw that shit out in the fuckin' dirt. She is not allowed to set foot through that front door."

"Goddamn, Dad. That's fuckin' great! Ha ha ha ha!"

"Yeah, fuck that. Don't take no shit."

And then he got back to cooking his chorizo.

So I did like the old man said, dumped her shit in the dirt, went to hock a loogey and right when the spit exited my mouth—the *second* I did it—I looked up and there she was walking down the sidewalk (we live on the corner) right in front of my house.

That spit landed on her blue dress that sat in the dirt. I cracked a smile, and turned to the door.

She didn't try to stop me.

She didn't call my name.

She looked like a corpse in that tight black vintage dress of hers.

Sometimes my old man—he really knows what to do.

He gets it just right.

He knows best

afterall.

Viva Losbetos!

There are literally dozens of them in the valley.
Mexican food places
that end in "betos" or "bertos."
But for me
there was never any other
besides "Losbetos."
It sat at the crossroads of
Greenfield and University,
a few hundred feet from my dad's house.
Growing up through my teen years,
it was always a part of my routine.
It was always there.
I took great pride in that place,
always pledging my love
for their immaculate burros.
Bean & Cheese or
beans, lettuce, rice, and cheese.
The Country Burro, with eggs, potatoes, and cheese.
That's what I would order from that place.
I'd walk in and the owner,
(who was always working
in his jeans and Losbetos' shirt
and the fancy leather belt with a shiny Mexican buckle)
he'd always say,
"Bean & Cheese or Country?"

From my days with Ian as dirty punkers,
carrying back our brown bags of burros,
to being married, living at my dad's,
my walks to Losbetos
afforded much needed breaks
from my pregnant and moody new bride.

Then years later,
when I was down & out,
3 bucks and some change to my name,
I'd spend it there and it was always worth it.

The cheese was melted,
the beans tasted like my nana's,
the tortillas were fluffy and soft,
putting Filibertos to shame.
Every woman that has danced with me
and then exited my life
went through there.
Once, over a three-day period,
I went in there with a new woman every day.
On the fourth I went in alone.
The owner's round face lit up
and he laughed loudly
as I approached the counter in my boots & leather jacket,
"No girls today, my fren?"
"Ha ha ha! No, no, not today."
It was like going home
every time I walked in.

I made friends with the owner's son
and we'd always bullshit
about our dads and how nothing pleased them.
He even hooked me up with a few Losbetos' hats
for preferred customers only.
I had it made.

Until last week:
life falling apart—
woman left me
job fired me
no money for the bus to job hunt.
I was stuck.
But that night I was with a friend
and he said he'd buy us burritos.
So we pulled up from the back
and I instantly sensed something wrong.
The family's SUV was parked in the drive-thru,
the sign shut off and darkened
and a big orange U-Haul parked next to the side door.
It felt like pulling up to your house
with yellow tape surrounding it.
Without saying a word,

I jumped from the truck and ran
straight for the back door.
When I saw inside,
my worst fears came to life,
my heart sank into my gut.
The room was empty,
everything moved out.
Only lines on the walls from where
the prep table used to be.
The owner and his son
were sweeping up
while the little niños ran around
with smiles on their faces.
But none of the adults were smiling.
Not one.
"Wha—? What's going on? Everything okay?"
I asked, hoping they were
just moving out old equipment
or something.
"No bro. We're closing down, homey,"
the son said to me, with a glum look.
"What? No. Why?"
"They raised the rent on us, can't pay it,
we're not making as much as we used to."
I felt guilty,
I hadn't eaten there in nearly two weeks.
"So that's it? You guys are done?" I asked.
The son looked to his dad and asked him in Spanish.
He told him and then he told me,
"We're gonna try and find another location with cheaper rent,
but I don't know. We'll see."
Then he gave me his number
and I said goodbye,
walked back out to the truck
where my friend was waiting.
"Goddamn, dude. You look like a family member just died."
"Yeah, that's what happened. Basically."
Goddamnit.
I'm gonna starve now.

Even though it was pouring rain outside,
I rode the bus to Tempe anyways,
desperate to get out of the house.
Dressed in my most typical looking
greaser cliché clothing imaginable—
black leather jacket,
motorcycle boots,
jeans,
and a plain black t-shirt—
I headed out.

Got off the bus
and had to piss,
so I walked up to a bar . . .
if you could call it that . . .
Bahama Frank's or some cartoony shit.
My greasy hair was falling in my face,
so I combed it back into place
and put the comb away
before opening the door.
The instant I stepped inside,
the opening chords to
"Bad to the Bone" by George Thorogood
BLARED over the speakers in the bar.
"Da na na nah nu . . ."
The entire room of blonde, Docker-wearing, Polo-shirted,
bleached all-gleaming white teeth shining in the too well-lit, fran-
chised-themed bar erupted in at my entrance
"HEEEEEEYYYYYYYYY! FONZE!" someone yelled.
"STAY GOLD, PONYBOY!"
More laughter.
I went back out in the rain
and pissed behind the building of the bar.
One of the Mexican dishwashers came out to throw the trash.
He saw my dick.
He laughed too.

Most will say that Punk broke in 1977,
but if you ask me they're about twenty years off.
In 1954 Elvis Presley toured the southern United States
and changed the face of music forever.

Every night, in every town, someone important was in the audience watching, mesmerized by this punk kid with greasy hair and loud & crazy clothes. Seeds were planted at every show and by 1955 Rockers were born.

Buddy Holly
Jerry Lee Lewis
Roy Orbison
Gene Vincent
Eddie Cochran
Johnny Cash
the list goes on and on.

They watched that hillbilly on the stage
and they thought, *I could do that too.*

After that, the floodgates opened up, Rock 'n' Roll was set loose upon the country. Greasy-haired, pill poppin', reefer smokin', side-burned delinquents toured the country, got on television and the world was never the same.

Elvis was banging girls, three at a time, and moving out of the Memphis ghetto.

Gene Vincent & The Blue Cats were trashing hotel rooms
and pulling guns on old ladies while driving a Cadillac backwards down the street at 2 a.m.

Buddy Holly & Little Richard were double-teaming a groupie in the dressing room as the announcer called Buddy to the stage.

Chuck Berry was fucking white, blond, teenage girls in the back of the car he slept in.

Eddie Cochran introduced everybody to reefer at house parties in Hollywood while strumming his guitar and singing "C'mon Everybody."

But the music—my Elvis—led the first rebellion, the first revolt of America's youth.

The visceral sting of that Rockabilly guitar, the sex beat of the drums—it did what it was supposed to do. The kids all rocked, rioted, and rolled, ripping up theater seats, pulling down the red velvet ropes and defying the racial barriers, uniting them all, black & white, while the old mummies, the squares, read the headlines in horror.

They had wild hairstyles & long sideburns; wore bright and flashy clothes; and none of them gave a shit about anything but getting their kicks, rockin' and rollin', and doing whatever they wanted.

And like the Punk Rock of the late 1970s, the movement was over in a matter of five years.

By 1960, Elvis had his ducktail shaved off by Uncle Sam, returning as a tanned crooner.

Jerry Lee Lewis was ruined by the teenage-cousin sex scandal.

Little Richard gave up Rock 'n' Roll to become a preacher.

Chuck Berry sat in jail for statutory rape, while the Beach Boys stole his songs.

Johnny Cash was drugged out and losing it.

Buddy Holly, Ritchie Valens, The Bopper, and Eddie Cochran—all dead.

Gene Vincent survived the crash that killed Eddie, but he lost his mind, holding imaginary conversations in his dressing room with his dead best friend.

They all lived fast and paid the price long before Dee Dee Ramone, Henry Rollins, Joe Strummer, and all the rest got their turns at Rock 'n' Roll rebellion.

Punk Rock, Rockabilly, Rock 'n' Roll—it's the same shit.

It's rebellion.

So think twice

before you roll your eyes

and call it fucking dinosaur music.

Smile and Dial

Lunch time at the call center—
it's a fuckin' madhouse.
They let all sixty employees go at once.
I don't know why,
but they do.
Dozens stand in line
at the three microwaves
waiting their turn to zap their shitty frozen foods—
Salisbury steaks,
mac 'n' cheese,
hot pockets.
They laugh,
"Goddamn, it's like I'm waitin' in line at the DMV or some shit."
Then they race
to wolf down their food
so they can fit in a cigarette
before their thirty minutes are up.

A table of lonely fat girls
share a large pizza
and eyeball every man that walks by.

The Blacks eat leftover Church's Chicken
and tuna with crackers.

The Mexicans have their leftover carne asada
from the cookout of last weekend.

You can hear about their lives.
In between each bite
they talk
about the public health insurance
they no longer qualify for
and the food stamps
that are about to be cut off.
Every man there has his *she* story.
"My baby's mama, *she* don't even let me see my kids."
They talk about how *she* hates them

for ruining her life, her tits, and her body altogether.
But the hate runs deep on both sides.

Outside the breakroom is where they all smoke.
It's a patio area
of caged-in fences.
Metal bars run along the ceiling.
One of the girls reaches up,
grabs one of the bars
and does some fancy shit.
Stripper acrobatics.
I'd seen the move before
and it made me happy
to know that the lady got out
and found a new line of work;
selling your body pays a lot better
than selling your voice.

Then
a black & white squad car pulls up out front.
Its mere presence
stirs everyone up
on the smokers' patio.
They all think it's for them
'cause they all have their reasons.
"Shit, I got overdue fines!"
"Fuck, I knew that bitch was gonna turn my ass in
for that child support."
"I got warrants. I'll be in the bathroom, Elvis."
We watched two officers step out
(two butchy female cops with
spiky hair, gel melting
and running down
like dripping liquid sideburns)
and head inside.
"Oh damn! Them butch cops are da worst, my nigga."
"Yeah, they don't fuck around. Slam you ass
to the pavement in a heartbeat, you better believe that shit!"
Three of my buddies emerged from a smoke-filled car,
eyes redder than the Devil's dick,
stinking of malt liquor and Mexican brickweed.

"What's going down, Elvis?" they ask.
Paranoid.
Not taking their eyes off
the black & white parked out front.
"Don't know. Two of 'em just went inside. They're looking for
somebody . . ."
"Goddamn."
My mind drifted to my own
overdue traffic fines and
back pay child support.
My Black Cloud.
The officers walked back out
and drove away.
Empty-handed.
Then there was
laughter,
smiles,
sighs of relief.
Everyone had been given a reprieve.
One more day
on the phones and under the radar.
For now.
Tomorrow could be different.

Everyone puts their cigarettes out
and heads back in.
They smile & dial—
just like the sign above their desk
tells them to.

We woke up,
my son and I,
got dressed,
ate cereal and got to work
helping the old man
clean and organize the garage.

I opened my father's treasured
bow & arrow case
to show my son.
I explained how it all worked,
while he listened intently.
Minutes later,
he had a wire coat hanger,
pretending it was a bow
shooting vampires.
I was the head vampire apparently.

The old man gave me $20,
told me to take Billy
to the barber Beasly
for a high and tight haircut.
"That boy's hair is out of fuckin' control."
True. His hair stuck out, all big and poofy.
Poor boy got his mother's hair.
We walked the mile together,
my son and I,
laughing and horsing around.
Over headphones, I played him that song
"Heavy Metal,"
the chorus being,
"CALL IT, HEAVY METAL!"
Billy looked up at me,
confused.
"Is he saying 'garlic heavy metal'?"
"Ha ha ha ha! No buddy . . .
'call it heavy metal' is what he's saying."

"Oh . . . I like garlic heavy metal better, Dad."
So he just kept singing his version
the whole way there.
I just kept laughing.
We got to the shop and I showed Billy the poem I wrote
about the barbershop.
Mr. Beasly got it printed on some
fancy yellow paper,
framed it,
and hung it on the wall
next to a shadowbox of old straight razors.
Billy's eyes were wide
and beaming with pride.
"I wanna grow up to write stories too Dad."
With his fresh haircut
and a smile on his face,
I bought us lunch and we walked back.
We worked on his homework for a while,
then went back outside to play.
"Spirit in the Sky"
played from the radio
as Billy did a zombie/skeleton dance
in the bed of my father's truck.

I was still pretty broken up
from my lady walking out on me
but,
at that moment in time, I acknowledged a reality.
If she were still here,
she'd be sitting in the bedroom
watching TV
while I spent time with my son & my dad.
She'd text me,
"Are you gonna spend any time with me today?"
But she was gone.
Everyday
I'm more and more
okay with it all.
Hey,
one less fuckin' thing to worry about.
Right?

I'll keep telling myself this
until it becomes my
truth
fact
law
gospel.
Shout it from the rooftops!
Go tell it on the mountain!

Part Six

Purgatorium

Five years. Five years of this shit. Five years of 120 degree summers, standing at bus stops and pouring sweat, my pomade melting down my forehead, holes in my shoes and the ass torn open in my jeans from the inner thigh to the back.
Five years of:

"Hey man, you should come out tonight."

"The buses stopped running at 9 o'clock. Can you pick me up?"

"Fuck man, I would . . . but you live so far out there."

And it's not just that I don't have a car. No. That wouldn't be too bad, I'd actually have a fighting chance. No, what I don't have is a license, and I know what you're thinking . . . It wasn't from a DUI or anything serious. *Nope.* It was something totally stupid and completely my fault.

Five years ago I was a newly single/free man after splitting with the wife, driving around in my Honda Accord, dating girls from bars . . . going wherever I pleased and thinking of starting a band. Then one day I got pulled over and ticketed for driving with an expired registration. The officer told me to go to emissions and just get a new one. So I tried that. At emissions they told me that I had an electrical issue in the dashboard, so my car wouldn't pass. They said I needed to take it to a mechanic and get it fixed before I could get the tags. The mechanic said it was gonna be upwards of six hundred dollars, money I didn't have. At the time I was working in a group home for the developmentally disabled, caring for human beings and getting minimum wage. Every dollar I got I needed just to stay above water, keep gas in my tank and food in the fridge. So six hundred dollars might as well have been a million to me. And it wasn't like I was gonna stop driving the car. I had to get to work. I accumulated one ticket after another, all, except one, in the city of Mesa. Back then, I was completely ignorant of bus lines. (It wouldn't be for long, though, before I'd know them intimately.)

Against my better judgement I took a girl out to the movies, paid for everything—even drove her home all the way to Scottsdale. On the way home I got pulled over and ticketed. *Again*. That made the fourth one and I knew the jig was up.

I couldn't even make it to my court date in Scottsdale. I couldn't drive, didn't know the bus lines, and no one could give me a ride. So, because I was a no-show, my license was suspended and they put me in default status, which meant I'd have to pay the fine, in full—$2,643.12—paid before the suspension could be lifted. And that's just in Scottsdale. I still owe over $1,400 to Mesa before THAT suspension can be lifted.

So for five years it's been the same minimum wage jobs:
the call centers,
the auto glass shops,
the day programs for the disabled,
the food service shit.

And about half of them I either lost or came close to losing because of the goddamn buses. Sometimes they just don't show up. It's cost me more jobs than I care to remember. The shitty thing is, and here's the kicker, I can't get a higher paying job because I don't have a dependable vehicle, but I can't get a car without the high paying job and I rip at my hair and I froth at the mouth sobbing and crying sometimes, feeling like I'm stuck on a desert island of dirt, rock, and cactus—stuck and doomed, damned to these barren desert streets. It makes dating a real pain in the ass.

No chick wants to drive all the way out to where I'm at, away from the cool side of town near Tempe or Phoenix where they live. And the ones I've lived with, oh jesus, that's worse. At first they're fine with driving me places now and then or dropping off my son with his mother every Sunday. Then one day like an egg cracking, they just get sick of it. And they start to resent me for not having a license, for not having a car. But their resentment ain't got nothing on my own resentment for myself. Because every year that passes, with each one there's a new hope—some way, some scheme, some scam and I think I'll be able to save up enough money to buy my life back. But each time I'm actually able to save up my dough, something horrible happens: my girlfriend's car breaks down and we need the money to fix it. *Watch it go*. Or when I got the advance for this book that was supposed to pay for my fines: *Gone*. Then I lost my job and that money was needed for (where the money always disappears to) rent, gas for my girl's car, food, electricity. Uncle Sam finally gave me something: money for school. I had a little over a grand left after my class was paid for. It seemed like a sure thing. I just had to get a ride to the courthouse. That day I got kicked out of my Dad's house, wound up sleeping on a twin bed in my mother's crowded apartment.

Then I found this place for rent. That money was what got me into this trailer. It gave me this life that I have now, which really is great except for this one little giant thing. Not being able to just get in my car, go pick up my son from school, take him to the arcade, and drop him off at his mom's. This may sound simple to you, silly even, but it's my greatest dream. Until then I'm confined to this strip of sidewalk between Guadalupe and Elliot just off Gilbert Road. I can only go as far as my feet will take me. My Converse shoes and my father's cowboy boots all had holes in the soles, so I bought a pair of Saucony running shoes last week. And now, shit, now, I walk so fast and so hard, hell, I've started running.

You'll see, I'm gonna stick to this. Keep running, keep typing because for the first time in a long time it feels like it's taking me somewhere. Like I could be close to finally paying this shit off, reclaiming my independence and dignity and driving far away from this desert island of rock, dirt, and cactus.

But, then again, I say this every year.

Remember?

It's always something.

Within twenty-four hours everything changed. The old man kicked me out again, so I was back in that twin-sized bed surrounded by my mother's boxes & plastic bins, my clothes in big piles with the hangers left in, just dying for a home.

But the day I got kicked out, I got the call, the one I didn't think would ever come. It was for a transcription job doing reality t.v. shows, typing what cast members said in the interview room. Word for word. Every burp, fart, and stutter is transcribed, using a foot pedal to stop, play, rewind, and fast forward.

The caller asked me to come in for an interview the next day, but then called me right back saying she had someone call out sick.

"Fuck the interview. Do you just wanna start? Like . . . today?"

So I went in that day and got typing.

The office was located in a 1960s trailer in the middle of a small trailer park, next to a little house. The boss, a middle-aged Rasta lady with straight brown hair and kindly face, turned out to also run the trailer park.

I asked her about one of the trailers with a "For Rent" sign, the only one available in the whole lot of seven trailers. She said it was a one bedroom and less than $500 a month. Two days later I got a few hundred bucks that I had been waiting on from my financial aid. It was my only way out, my only way in. After I paid the move-in expenses I only had $13 to my name, but it was all right because my good luck just kept on rolling. I found a $200 balance on my food stamp card. At the end of the day, my face hurt from smiling so big, for so long.

Now I have a porch that's mine, Mason jars with ice water, good food in the fridge. Best of all, it's only a short walk across the trailer park to get to work everyday.

My Rasta boss landlord lady has two little boys around my son's age. Since we moved in, all he's done is play outside with them, running around with rocks, sticks, dirt, and random objects—the way kids are supposed to play. I almost can't type this, can't put into words what this means to me. No more father looming over me or mother yelling my name. To know I can step out onto my porch at night and see the Gilbert water tower lit up in white light, or take in the scent of Joe's Real BBQ blowing in the breeze adds a gleam to even the most gloomy day. I can walk the downtown streets with its old west, wooden awnings hanging overhead. Visit the old tyme tattoo shop with its old-style custom flash, or stop in at the wooden, two-window, one-door front of my Dad's former bar, The Mustang Lounge, where I watched him sling drinks, while I played the entertainment trivia touch screen while sipping Shirley Temples.

But the best part, and it's such a simple thing, is to walk the sidewalks (stamped AA Beardon, 1930) of my new neighborhood with my son. It's everything I've ever wanted and it's just dumb luck—to find a job and a home in one fell swoop like this.

I'm on a writer's retreat where I practice typing all day at my job and then cook myself dinner at sundown. T-Bone Walker's voice fills my little trailer as I take in sunsets from my porch and lean against the railing, a jar of ice water in my hand, my stomach full. I have that after-dinner smoke, grateful to not have a care in the world, knowing the next cigarette

and

the next page are here.

Finally.

I can put my feet up

and hold my head high.

I just watched
Robert Rodriguez's little-known
Greaser-trash epic
Road Racers
and now it's got me
fiending
for a Rockabilly guitar—
the fuzzier
the dirtier
the better.
I ain't talking about no "Teddy Bear."
Nah.
I'm talking about screams.
Shaky, jumpy, nervous, vocals
like Charlie Feathers
or Bloodshot Bill . . .
the real outsider shit
for degenerate Rock 'n' Roll fiends.
The radio doesn't sound the same,
they're playing soulless airwaves and I can't stand it.
I'm a rocker and I wanna rock.
I shaved my head four months ago
and the hair is finally long enough,
just barely long enough,
to be able to comb.
When I got off work yesterday,
I practically ran to the drug store
for my first can of pomade in four months.

I stood in my chonies,
in front of a door-length mirror,
Ricky Nelson's "Teenage Idol"
filling the white bathroom,
running that comb
up and out,
getting the part on the side
hairline perfect.

I spent over an hour
standing there
rubbing the pomade inbetween my fingers,
getting it all heated up
and slicking it into my hair,
combing it through.
I couldn't stop smiling.
A weight had been lifted from my shoulders.
I could breathe again.

I woke up to my pillowcase this morning,
greasy once again,
and I couldn't have been happier.
It might sound silly to you
but for me
it's an essential thing.
It is me.
I don't know why I'm like this,
but I never really think about it.
Some things just are.

When I walk to the store,
it's a joke,
and everybody laughs.
Cars pass me and
sometimes I notice their reactions.
Most often someone sees me,
laughs,
taps the driver on the shoulder
then they both look and start laughing.
Sometimes the window rolls down,
and they yell something,
but I've got ear buds in and
Lemmy is growling Eddie Cochran's lyrics
and they can't say shit.
They can say it.
They can shout it.
But I'm not listening
because I'm rubber
and because they're glue.
I just get to do whatever the fuck I want.

All the time.
It's really cool,
man
and I like it fine,
except for one thing.
Just one thing I don't like
is that I never get to leave.
I just keep walking Gilbert Road,
both sides,
back and forth
and that's it.

I don't know how I'm ever gonna have wheels.
It didn't used to bother me too much,
but the older I get, the more it gets under my skin.
There's a classic car dealership
on my walk to the store
and it's just torture
because to be in an old car,
listening to that music,
the hot summer wind stinging my face—
that's my fantasy,
my wildest dream,
and it's so fucking simple.
So why can't I touch it?

Up All Night

I'm outside on the porch again,
and the heat's burning me
and the cigarettes keep getting smoked.
Somehow, still,
even in this burning heat,
I wanna blow out smoke.
The cold, painful, black & grey winter
has passed.
Every morning
I drink creamer & sugar with coffee.
I made it through and
I'm fine now.

Organizing the stories
for the book,
getting the front & back covers
all layed out.

Got a raise at work.
I'm a valued member of the team.
I continue to transcribe
the latest and greatest
reality TV has to offer.
Sitting in rolled up jeans
and no shirt,
laughing and cracking jokes with my co-workers,
just spacing out while
typing the mindless drool
of rich fools—
the days go quickly—

Painted the trailer
mint and white,
making my own little white trash palace.

Yeah, the summer's here.
The living is easy.

After work
I take a slow walk to fill the jugs with water.
Shirtless,
headphones in,
smoking a cigarette,
and smiling in the oven-like air,
I bask in the hairdryer breeze of an Arizona summer.
I haven't got a care in the world
and I live in one pair of blue jeans.

The nighttime is always something else now.
I rarely sit alone
like I used to.
My typewriter hasn't had an ink ribbon in it
for four months.

I'm just hanging out with an old friend
or my new lady.
Usually the lady.
She's always over here now
and I ain't complaining.
And we laugh our asses off,
eat burritos,
talk in funny voices,
geek out about Rockabilly music,
kiss on each other,
sneak into a live Patsy Cline show,
(taking a seat in the very back row),
hold hands, smile, and laugh
over a candlelit table,
have sex in the backseat of her car
with the blue glow from the radio in the dash,
Gene Vincent crooning "Summertime"
and its feeling perfect.

It seems like this whole summer is gonna be
an all-nighter,
diving in headfirst,
giving it all we got,
taking in the desert skies and
getting lost staring into a campfire,
falling asleep as the windows begin

to glow blue with the morning dawn,
going somewhere,
anywhere,
and doing whatever we please
because
it's summertime
and the living is easy.

Tattoos (Roadmaps & Flashlights)

I got my first tattoo at seventeen,
but it started much earlier for me.
I had grown up
seeing them all around me.

At six years old,
I sat in the living room
of my dad's best friend's house,
playing Super Mario 3
while "Uncle Mike" got tattooed at the kitchen table
with a portrait of his daughter, Chelsea—
which still looks picture perfect to this very day.

Then there was my Uncle Ralphie
and five women's names
down his arm.
One for each major love.

But really it was my mother . . .
After the divorce,
she went all out . . .
cowgirl, tequila-pounding, tattoo-getting,
2 a.m. burrito-eating,
wild woman.
When she got her first tattoo
of a small unicorn on her shoulder,
my grandmother openly wept tears of shame.
But when I was ten,
my mom went for another tattoo . . .
the face of a Jaguar on her ass.

Holding her hand,
walking past the walls
of tattoo flash:
grim reapers, skulls, snakes, dragons, devils,
I was in awe.
I didn't know where to look first.
There was so much a ten-year-old boy

couldn't help but love.
The tattoo artist was Michael Bacon,
a handsome blonde dude
that looked like he could've been Kevin Bacon's cousin.
He was buddies with tough-guy actor Michael Madsen
and had worked on a few Hollywood movies
doing make-up and tattoos.
When I saw his tattoo
on his upper right arm
of Wolverine from X-Men
ripping through the skin
with his Adamantium claws,
my jaw dropped.
"You can get stuff that's NOT on the walls?!" I asked.
Michael chuckled,
"Yeah, kid. Of course you can.
Just about anything you can think of, you can get tattooed."
Seven years later,
—and I was heavy into Punk,
'80s Hardcore Punk,
like Black Flag & Minor Threat—
I came home from school one day
and my mom was in her room
smoking a cigarette and pacing around,
obviously excited about something.
"Hey mijo, you wanna get a tattoo?"
"What?"
"Yeah, I got a guy that'll do it
even though you're not eighteen yet."
I didn't pause to think about it.
"Yeah, of course, Ma."
"Well, get on the computer
and print out what you wanna get . . ."
I almost got The Misfits' Crimson Ghost logo,
but at the time
I was heavy into the band Minor Threat
and the "straight edge" idea,
which meant don't drink, don't smoke, don't do drugs.
Coming from a long line of alcoholics,
it was my best way to rebel
like I never had.

We went and the guy was really scummy.
For sixty bucks and a bottle of pain pills,
he tattooed just the words: "xStraightEdgex" on my back.

After I turned eighteen,
when I had the money,
I started making appointments
with Michael Bacon,
getting portraits of my favorite
horror movie slashers:
Jason, Michael Myers, Leatherface.

I couldn't stop listening to "Die, Die, My Darling" by The Misfits;
so at my desk at the call center,
I drew up a design
of a coffin with a banner that read, "Your Future"—
as in the line, "Your future's in an oblong box."
The guy that tattooed that one for me
is a bit of local legend
when it comes to
shitty tattooing.
Dozens of local punks got stuck
with some shitty tattoos,
others got cover-ups.
He tattooed me and my stoner buddy Kyle
in the kitchen
with a bottle of Wild Turkey in my lap,
my straight-edge days behind me.
It was on the soft fleshy part of the inner arm
so I jumped a bit at one point.
You can still see the line straying away
and out.

When I finally got my Black Flag bars,
it was on my 22nd birthday.
My buddy had offered to tattoo me for free
on the floor of his bedroom.
He wore a white, sailing captain's hat.
Two weeks later, the feds kicked in his door
because some underage cunt got hepatitis
and pointed the finger at my ole pal in the captain's hat.

The day I got my "TCB"—
my Take Care of Business ink of honor—
my mother was staying in an RV park
and some guy next door
had been looking in her windows
and even putting his hands on her,
trying to feel her up.
My girlfriend drove me over to his place.
I knocked on his door,
and he answered smiling,
asking if he could fucking help me.
"Yeah, you can help me, Mister.
That woman next door is my fucking mother
and you put your hands on her again
or you keep staring at her,
you're gonna wake up
with me standing over your fucking bed.
You get me, old man?"
His mouth hung open and he stammered his words,
shaking in the doorway.

I had to wait for over three hours with T-Bird
at the tattoo shop that night.
It was one of those Friday the 13th tattoo specials.
You could choose from about 20 or 30 small designs
that all had a "13" somewhere in them
and the tattoo was only 13 bucks.
I saw a "TCB" design that had a 13 incorporated into it,
but I asked him to just make it a regular TCB,
I already had a 13 on the back of my neck,
and it brought nothing but trouble.
Wouldn't you think it bad luck
if you got that most unluckiest of numbers tattooed
and then in the next 3 days you lost your job
and knocked up your girlfriend?
I did, so I was fucking done with "13" tattoos.
One was plenty.

I was sitting on the toilet,
trying to shit,
having a bad trip on mushrooms

when my stare drifted to the tattoo of Elvis Presley's face
on my right forearm.
He told me that being on the toilet was a dangerous place
and I'd "better look out man."

When I met the woman of my dreams,
the perfect pin-up sent from the 1940s,
I got two hearts with an arrow piercing them
and a blank banner holding them together.
It was the damnedest thing,
the entire time I was with that woman
the two hearts were raised up
and bumpy,
something was wrong with it.
After she left,
the hearts smoothed right out.
I'm glad I left the banner blank,
but I know what it was supposed to say,
what it was gonna say,
and that I'm saving *just for me.*

I've got over 18 of them right now
and I'm planning on slowing down a bit.
Everyone my age is in such a rush to
get fully sleeved up,
and I think it's just silly.
They're tryin' to be hard.
I don't want to be fifty years old,
looking at my arms with only the shit I was into during my 20s.
I've got a lot of living to do.
I'm glad that I've done it slowly, over time,
sometimes going years without getting anything.
Every one I have is of
a different time,
a different place,
a different mindset,
a different me—
constantly evolving,
changing.
But the marks of the past never go away,
it's all building.

These tattoos
will someday serve as road maps,
a graphic history of my life,
a letter to my future self,
a flashlight in the dark
for when
my mind inevitably
lets go
and won't remember a fucking thing.
I've got my flashlight
and I'm adding to the roadmap as I go.
I didn't plan this trip,
but I'm sure as hell
making it,
not faking it,
definitely taking it
as far as I can go.

THE GROWN-UP INSIDE

I am a grown man
of twenty-six years
and yet still
sometimes when it storms
and the lightening
lights up the room,
and the thunder cracks
with deafening volume and power
even now
I get scared
for a second or two
and I feel like that little boy again.
For that brief moment
I want to get close to someone
who will keep me safe and protect me.
But then I remember,
at my age,
no one can save me
anymore than I can save myself.
We're all just hunkering down,
riding out this storm we've all been dropped into,
riding it out the best we can.
But eventually
you see
we all go under the dark waters
into the black
of the unknown.
The only comfort for me
is that we must all go through it.
Anyone that ever was, is, or will be,
we all get our turn.
So don't worry,
I tell myself.
Relax.
Everybody's doing it.

Fiction

"Are you sure about this? It seems kinda fuckin' weird Mike . . ."

"No man, she's totally cool. She likes it. I do this at least once a week."

Bobby was hesitant, but Mike insisted he try it out. There had been a big fire in one of the apartment buildings a few weeks ago, the only part left untouched was a storage room under the stairs. She lived in there, he said.

"Usually, you gotta call her on the prepay first . . . like before you go over. But, for me . . . see I'm a regular, so she just gave me a key."

"What, so you just go inside?"

"Yeah, dude. Like I said, she likes it. Most of the time she's all doped up and like, passed out. But like, as long as, like, I show her the money . . . she just like, tells me to stick it in. She likes it, says it helps wake her up and shit. Really gets her going."

Mike was breathing hard, as he talked. They were getting close to the burned out building.

"I don't know man, this seems shitty. Fucking a junkie-hooker that lives under some stairs in a burned out building? I mean, what the fuck man? Let's just go home and fuck our wives."

Mike stopped walking and stood, staring at Bobby in disbelief. Slowly he spoke.

"That is . . . the stupidest thing . . . I have ever heard you say."

"How? This is . . ."

"This . . . is a fucking adventure goddamnit! A break from the day-to-day, a break from the norm, man. A taste of strange. Now c'mon already! We're almost there"

They slowly started walking again.

"Well . . . do other guys in the complex do it?" Bobby asked, kicking a rock.

"Of course man! She's got like six regulars a week. She's got that and like, all the guys that just try her once for the hell of it. She does group deals too. The girl like, fucked a bunch of the high school boys before. She told me about that. The state champion on the wrestling team even gave it to her."

It was amazing how the fire had blackened nearly every inch of the place. But that door beneath the stairs was still faded blue and white. They walked up to the little door.

"Alright, now . . . do you wanna go first or second?" Mike asked, fumbling his keys into the door.

"I don't know. We'll see man." Bobby didn't know if he was really gonna do it.

Opening the door, they found her asleep in a small recliner, *too* small, it looked like it was made for a child. All miniature and shit. Bobby thought she was gonna look like the Crypt Keeper in a tube top and heels. But to his surprise, she didn't look half bad. A real pretty little redhead in flannel pajama pants. She had painted black toenails and wore a Ramones t-shirt.

"What's her name?" Bobby asked, nervously thumbing his Levi's pocket.

"I dunno. Everyone just calls her 'Easy'."

Mike shook her, trying to wake her up. It kinda worked. She opened her eyes a centimeter, nodded, and mumbled,

" . . . go ahead, baby . . . zzzzzz . . ."

"Alright, buddy . . . I . . . am gonna go first," Mike said, stripping down.

Bobby leaned against the wall, between that and the arms of the mini recliner.

Three Dole banana boxes were stacked in the corner. Lubes, condoms, and punched out cigarette butts covered the top box. With his dick all shiny and lubed up, Mike put it in and got to it. It didn't take long, two minutes into it and he blew his load. She didn't move an inch.

"And don't say anything man! I usually go a lot longer."

"Hey, I wasn't gonna . . ."

"It's been a week since I fucked, so just shut up."

She twitched and snored. Track marks on the tops of her feet. Mike reached down and spread apart her pussy lips, looking up and smiling at Bobby.

"Well? Come on, dude . . . slip it in."

Bobby unzipped his pants and pulled them down to his ankles.

Somehow, his dick was hard. He tore open a ribbed condom from the pile of them on the stacked Dole boxes. Bobby slid the condom down his shaft. The room stunk like a can of expired tuna. Mike was still holding open her pussy lips.

"Mike. Move your hands. Come on, I got it man . . ."

208

He did like he was asked and stepped to the side, stroking himself and grinning big. Bobby slid it in with ease, and began pumping away. Easy moaned with pleasure, at last waking up, her eyes finally open, and looking at who was fucking her.

"Give it to me, Daddy. Give it. Fuck me good."

When Bobby finally came, five minutes later, Easy was wide awake. Bobby rolled the condom off and held it in his hand.

"Do you have a garbage . . . Miss Easy?"

Mike and Easy both cracked up laughing.

"No. Just throw it behind something. Anywhere, I don't give a shit," she said.

Feeling a bit embarrassed, he quickly put his clothes back on. Mike stood, still naked, lighting a smoke for himself and one for Easy too. They were both smiling rotten-toothed grins. All Bobby wanted was to get home to his wife, the guilt and shame already eating him up. Easy laughed exhaling her cigarette.

"Shit. That was just what I needed. Thanks guys. Make him a copy of the key, would ya Mike?" she said with a hearty, smoker's cackle.

Bobby stood with his hand on the doorknob.

"See? I told you, Bobby . . . she likes it."

My mom needed something from the store, so I told her I'd walk up there for her and get it. We were barely getting by, the two of us. She was living on a disability check and I was inbetween jobs. Again. So these little walks to the store were all I had.

I got her Epsom salts and was walking back, had just walked past the hardware store, when a small, sleek, black BMW pulled up next to me. To my surprise it was a chick—a big-titted redhead with pink sunglasses. There was something in her eyes when she peeked below the sunglasses. I saw something in them that frightened me. A voice inside was screaming at me *just keep walking, just keep walking!*

But like a fool, I ignored it and bent over the passenger seat, into the convertible that smelled new.

"How big is your cock?" the lady asked, her chest heaving and jiggling with every breath she took and every word she spoke.

"What?"

"I said . . . how big is your cock?"

"Ha ha!" I took a look around, expecting to see a hidden camera or a film crew in a van across the street. There was no one. No witnesses. I leaned back down, "7 inches? Maybe 8? I don't know lady, I haven't measured my dick since the 11th grade!"

The redhead took off her sunglasses completely and I watched her bright green eyes scan me from my worn-out Converse to the greasy pompadour on my head. It took an eternity.

I grew uncomfortable just standing there, squirming while the redheaded fox continued to inspect me.

"Okay. Get in. Hurry up."

I wasn't thinking, just reacting to it all. I'd always dreamed of this when I was walking down that same old motherfuckin' street—the only street that I ever saw. Always dreaming of being discovered by a beautiful woman in a sports car. And now here she was. Here *we* were, driving down the street, the breeze blowing through our hair. She made an immediate right turn onto a suburban side street and parked in front of a house with a "For Sale" on the front lawn.

Again she took off the sunglasses. "Let me see it," she said, staring at my crotch.

"Whoa, whoa, lady. What's this all about?"

"My husband and I . . . we have certain . . . tastes. Things we like, things we enjoy. He's an older guy, so he likes to watch young guys fuck me. I mean, just really give it to me good, make me scream. And of course after your services have been . . . rendered . . . you'll be paid two thousand dollars. Now do you think you can do that?"

"Uh . . . I—I think so."

"Well, I need you to know so. And if you were bullshitting me, if that cock isn't at least 7 inches, you can get out of the car right fucking now."

"No it is, it is."

"Well . . ."

"Well . . . you gotta start my engine first—"

Before I could finish my cheesy line, she flipped into the passenger seat, climbing on top of me.

"Rip it open," she said, looking down.

I did as I was told and ripped the front of her blouse open, the buttons flying in all directions, bouncing off the windows and rolling on the dashboard. Her two, round, fake tits sprang out of the top, hitting me in the face as she rubbed them up and down and all around.

She kissed me sloppily and then started in with some biting bullshit. She met my lip so hard, it drew blood.

Acting purely on reflex, I grabbed her by the arms very hard and pulled her back from me and stared at her with those crazy, intense eyes that I sometimes got when startled.

"Oh . . ." she said, looking down at the hard on in my Levi's. "Alright. You wanna see the house?" she asked.

I let go of her arms and she rolled off me, hopping into the driver's seat and starting the car up. She drove all the way to the edge of the city where the Red Mountains in the east meet the long winding road out of town and into the desert.

It was a large ranch-style mansion decorated with cowboy themed shit. The redhead parked the sports car in a massive garage filled with dozens of rare and expensive automobiles.

She told me to leave my plastic grocery bag of Epsom salts in the car. She said I could get it later, when we were done.

I followed her to an elevator at the back of the garage. We took it all the way down to the very bottom. Stepping out of the elevator, I found myself in a large, expansive grey room. The concrete floors

were shiny and slick and reminded me of the floor in the meat department at the job I had just lost.

The room had a few beds in it. Some custom-built sets were erected all over the room:

—an office,

—a jail cell,

—a medieval dungeon,

—a medical examination room.

There were several little sets built all over in the back of the room. I noticed the pitch black corners covered in darkness. I wondered what they had over there.

"So what do we do?" I asked, fidgeting in my pants, thumbing my switchblade stiletto in my right front pocket.

"We have to wait for my husband to come down. I just texted him."

"Oh, okay."

"You should take your clothes off and put this on," the redhead said, taking a hospital gown from a hanger next to the medical examination set.

". . . put that on and I'm gonna go get into character," she said, walking behind a white privacy screen, the old kind, like they used to have in doctors' offices. I undressed myself and got into the hospital gown.

I can't say what it was exactly, but I still had that nauseous, nervous feeling. I couldn't ignore it. So I hid my switchblade on me. Put it in the waistband of my underwear. And that made me feel a little safer. This whole thing was beyond belief. I was never this lucky so there had to be something rotten in Denmark. I could feel it in my bones. But there was no backing out now. I was riding this all the way. No choice.

I took a seat on the medical examination table, the thin paper crunching loudly beneath my ass. They had it down to the finest detail. Even the little slots with the *Highlights* magazines.

I stared at the black & white clock on the wall. It took them 28 minutes to finally come out—the two of them together. The tall, beautiful redhead and her rich old man. But they matched in an odd way. His face was nearly the same color as her hair, indicating a red-faced, big-nosed drinker. I'd seen that face a thousand times. Ain't no mistakin' it. He had white hair all

spiked up like how young people have it, and he wore nothing but gold. All over himself. Gold necklace, full fists of rings, bracelets. I couldn't fucking believe it. I tried not to laugh. I just snorted to myself. The cocksucker even dangled a Mercedes medallion around his neck, like Flavor Flav or something, it was that flamboyant.

But the guy was like 70 years old. None of it made any fucking sense. The florescent lighting above did this thing to his eyes. They appeared so sunken in that it created two black shadows where his eyes should've been—just coal black, endlessly hollow and empty. Those eyes, along with his red face recreated Satan himself, covered in gold and diamonds.

"What's up?" he said, extending his well tanned, leathery claw.

"Hey."

"Alright, so let's not waste any time. Let's get down to business. Huh?"

"Yeah, sure," I said.

"Fuck yeah! Let's fuck! You wanna fuck him, baby?"

"Why do you think I got him? Hell, I almost fucked him on the way home."

"Did you now?" he said, looking over at me with this look. I couldn't tell if it was pleasure or rage.

"Alright, alright then."

The chick started to walk up the three little steps of the examination table, her feet pale as snow and her toes, shiny and red like a paint job on a brand new Cadillac in 1956.

She climbed on top of me. Started kissing me and rubbing my dick under the examination gown.

From the corner of my eye I saw the husband moving closer to the camera, which was set up a few feet away. Looked to be hi-def shit.

She bit my lip again, really fucking hard. So hard, she pulled a big chunk of skin off.

"Goddamnit!" I yelled.

"What?" the husband shouted back.

"He hates it when I bite him!" the redhead shouted with a smile, blood on her lips from mine.

"Well, don't take any shit, son! If she does that again, you just give her a good smack!"

"What?"

"Yeah, don't be timid boy! This ain't fuckin' Sunday school! We're fuckin' here!"

She did it again. Without thinking of what that old coot was yelling about, I just hit her on principle, with a good open-handed smack across the cheek.

"There ya fuckin' go! That's what I'm talkin' about." The old man threw his hands in the air and started doing this little dance shit, the weirdest I had ever seen.

The redhead grabbed my face with her hands. Taking my eyes off the old man, who was now singing some song and shuffling around the floor.

Her mint-colored eyes met mine. She whispered to me, "I'm sorry," as she pulled me in and kissed me, then grabbed my hands to her breasts and proceeded to kiss me again, like a long lost love, not some guy off the street.

And that's the last thing I remember—besides the prick of the needle in my neck—just her red hair hanging in my face, the florescent light shining through.

When I came to, I was standing upright, but strapped to a table. My arms, my legs, my head, every part of me strapped down tight. I wasn't going anywhere. This was that bad feeling I got when she looked at me. This was where it ended. Right now.

They both stood there, staring at me and smiling with drinks in their hands, the cameras rolling. They had multiple cameras set up. Some 80s techno played from an iPod dock.

"What? What are you gonna do?" I slurred, it was hard to talk.

"I know, I'm sorry. Okay, look. We both agree that you probably are owed an explanation, I mean . . . these being your last moments and all . . ." the redhead interrupted, looking at me as she had before. There was love in her eyes.

"Honey . . . remember what I said? About how there are things that we like and things that we enjoy? I'm sorry, but this is what we like."

"Snuff?" I managed to choke out. Just the sound of that word chilled my fucking blood.

"Yeah. Hey . . . son, let me tell ya . . . we're actually saving you a whole lot of heartache and disappointment. You weren't gonna go anywhere, you weren't going to accomplish anything. You'd work the same shit jobs, bouncing from one to the other, until you finally died of either booze or drugs."

"It's for the best, sweetie," the redhead said.

I'd love to tell you they left the room for a few minutes and I was able to free my hand, take the switchblade from my underwear, cut myself free and kill them both, then clean out their cash and diamonds from the safe. But this was no movie. Well, not the kind with a happy ending anyway.

That's when she walked over to the table and grabbed the knife. The song on the iPod changed and I instantly recognized it. It was *the* song. I never could explain why, but as a boy this song would come on the radio—this 80s electro song—and it always scared the shit out of me. Turned my stomach. I never knew why, but now it all made sense. That song would be the last thing I'd ever hear.

With the cameras rolling, the redhead gave me one more kiss. I closed my eyes and pretended. I pretended that she was a girl that loved me. That she was kissing me goodnight, sending me off with a smile. I just kept my eyes closed, squeezing them tight. I didn't feel the knife when she slit my throat right there in that flourescent-lit, slick, grey basement.

It didn't hurt. I didn't feel any pain. Just warmth from the blood flowing down the front of my neck and chest—pure warmth sliding down my body. I started to get light-headed as darkness descended. Very quickly. I could hear my heartbeat in sync with a high-pitched ringing in my ears.

The last thing I saw was the redhead standing above me. Luckily the husband had his head behind the camera so I didn't have his grotesque face as my last vision.

No. It was the redhead and those mint green eyes.

They never found my body. The couple put me through a wood chipper and fed my scraps to their dogs, after slicing off my biceps for dinner that night.

They went on doing this for years, picking up guys and girls from the streets who were down on their luck and wouldn't be high profile, missing persons.

They acquired hundreds of DVD's, selling these snuff films to their elite and powerful friends in high places.

But they justified it all. Surely I wouldn't be missed. I didn't have a mother like they had a mother. I didn't laugh and love like they did. I was expendable. Disposable. Use once and discard. The rich eating the poor. I was blood-meal for their insatiable & gruesome appetites.

It's okay though. I'm not mad or anything now. It's just blackness. A dreamless sleep. I don't even know how I'm telling you this, but the worst part . . . the thing I still think about the most is my mother, and what she must of thought when her only son went to the store for Epsom salts and just never came back.

I know everybody says the same thing: "This was my first time," but it *really* was his first time. Alex had knocked up his girlfriend at just fifteen years old, and despite what everybody thought he was gonna do, he had stuck it out, done the honorable thing—the right thing.

They had just had their 10-year anniversary three weeks ago, celebrating at Olive Garden in relative silence, making a little small talk about the kids and work, but mostly they both just sat with their phones out, texting other people, more interesting people with new things to say. To say they had lost the spark, would've been an understatement.

They did have sex that night, but he didn't care if they did or didn't. He knew he wasn't missing much. Just the same old, same old: he on top doing all the work, and she just enduring his jack hammering until he could finally think of the girl from work and blow his load inside his wife. Then he'd roll off her, get back on his phone, back to texting while she sifted through episodes of Ru Paul's *Drag Race*, trying to find the one she missed.

"Who the fuck you talkin' to?"

"What the fucks it matter who I'm talkin' to?"

"Oh? Okay."

Her eyes squinted at the TV and he went back to texting, and when his guard was down, she snatched that phone up so fast.

"What the fuck?!"

Kalisha's eyes quickly, furiously, suspicously scanned the texts displayed.

"I'm talking to Felicia from work! Okay?!"

"Felicia?! Who da fuck is Felicia?! Uh huh!"

"Before you even trip, chill the fuck out. Okay? She's a fuckin' dyke."

"Yeah, sure she is . . ."

"Look, goddamnit!"

He brought up her Facebook page on the laptop. Her default picture was of her and her girlfriend captured in an embrace.

"See? C'mon baby, I wouldn't . . ."

"Motherfucker, don't start with your 'c'mon baby', bullshit. Whatever. Here," she said, tossing back the phone.

The truth was Felicia was *bi*sexual and she was, in fact, jocking Alex's shit. But at that point they'd only had a few movie dates.

The next night, while his wife thought he was working a swing shift at the call center, he actually had a movie date instead.

Alex and Felicia didn't go to the movie they were going to see that night, however. They got some food at a Hawaiian place and were walking up to the box office when she asked to go back to the car. Said she wanted to get her jacket.

"It gets cold as shit in that theater. They keep it like a goddamn meat locker in there."

"Yeah, I know. I'll get mine too."

Five minutes later they were in the back seat of the car, kissing each other and breathing hard, her hand moving back and forth over the hard-on in his jeans.

She pulled her titties out, they were big and plump, young and perky, jiggling and swaying with pierced nipples and a chest piece tattoo. They were much better than his wife's. After three kids, hers were deflated and saggy, with long & chewed-on nipples. Her tits depressed him, made him think of all the fine titties that he'd never squeeze, never taste, never see.

But here he was going outside his marriage, going out of his own moral boundaries, going for it— just going for it. They fucked right there in the back seat, under the cover of darkness in the vast movie theater parking lot, far back in the corner. Felicia's juices covered his crotch and got in between the crevices of his thighs.

Alex drove Felicia home and dropped her off, sealed with a kiss and the promise of more texts. When he got home his wife started in on him. She was suspicious and rightfully so. Alex was as guilty as a possum with a mouthful of bees.

"Where you been?"

"I told you baby . . . I was doing a swing shift at work."

"Yeah, nigga. A swing shift lasts eight hours. What the fuck you doing back after only five hours?"

He hadn't even thought of that. Fuck.

"I asked Steve and he said I could go early . . . I'm tired, baby. I couldn't stare at that screen anymo--"

His wife stared at him with a stone cold gaze, piercing right through his ass, before saying five words that made his blood run cold.

"Let me smell your dick."

"Wha--what?"

"Wha? Wh-what? You stuttering motherfucker. You heard me. Let me smell your dick!"

He knew his dick reeked of smelly pussy. He also knew his wife would cut his fucking dick off if she smelled it. He had to think quick.

And he did—the perfect bailout for the situation. He relaxed his asshole & his dick, then, just let it go. He pissed and shit his black denim pants. It only took a second before his wife could smell it, the hot shit now sitting in his drawers.

"Eww! What the fuck, Alex?!"

"See?! I didn't wanna tell you! Goddamnit!"

"Is that shit I smell? Is that fuckin' shit?!"

"Yeah! Okay?! Yeah! I shit myself! Okay? You caught me."

"Why?"

"I don't know why! I thought, it'd be fuckin' fun, ya know? Shitting my pants at work and having to come home early, then get yelled at by you for cheating or some bullshit."

His wife now looked genuinely concerned; her whole demeanor changed. "Baby . . . I'm sorry . . . look, just tell me . . ."

"Fuck this shit."

And Alex got in the shower, washed his shit-covered boxers in the shower, pushing clumps of shit down the drain with his fingers until every clump, every peanut was down the drain. His wife was laying in bed, waiting for him. He lay on his side and she curled up next to him, putting her arm over him, her body fitting against him like a locking puzzle piece, their fingers intertwining while she let out a heavy sigh.

"I'm sorry."

"It's okay."

"No, it's not. You're a good man. You always have been. You take care of me and these kids, you do everything. I know you would never do anything to jeopardize what we got. I know you're faithful and true to me. How could you not be? You're a good man."

"Yeah."

"Did you hear me, baby?"

She turned him over on his back and held his face in her hands, looking deep into his eyes—all the love she had on display for him. "You're a good man. And I love you."

Alex's eyes filled with tears. "I love you, too."

Then she kissed him.

Alex never cheated on her again. The guilt ate away at him slowly over the years, like a cancer devouring his thoughts on a daily basis. But he never told her. He loved her too much. Some things are better left unsaid. You just keep it to yourself. You curl up to it, hold it in your arms, in your head, and you suffer with it forever . . .

like a cactus teddy bear or something.

He woke up next to the empty spot where Wonder Woman had been, puked in the toilet, slammed down a forty-ounce Miller High Life and started putting on the suit: boots, the gray and black tights, the gloves, the yellow utility belt, and the cape (it was leather).

He put the cowl under his arm and left his apartment. It was a late start, nearly noon by the time the bus got him to Grauman's Chinese Theater.

He saw a lot of his friends and collegues as the bus pulled up to his stop. It was a regular day, all the characters were in their usual little groups:

Spiderman & Captain America, two Mormon boys that had been excommunicated from the church (after they got caught butt-fucking each other) were now stuck in Hollywood like everyone else.

The X-Men, or H-Men as most people called them, were a group of four junkies. One of them had a cousin at Fox and they got four replica X-Men costumes. So that's how they scored their junk everyday—garnered pretty good tips from the tourists too: Cyclops, Jean-Grey, Storm, and Wolverine. It was a good grift. Damn good idea.

Then you had the impersonators, plastic surgery freaks obsessed with Michael Jackson, or creepy bald men dressed as Dr. Evil. And there was always a lazy fat guy that would do Elvis. He wouldn't know any of the songs. So, instead, he'd spout the catch phrases all wrong, "Well, thank you, Ma'am . . . thank you so much." Those guys never lasted too long.

The cutesy cartoon characters were almost always pedophiles or old bag ladies. The horror people were, hands down, the most bat-shit insane of the lot. They got into the most fights and terrorized the kids and they talked a lot of shit and would bait guys into fights. Michael Myers would always start shit with guys that had beautiful women with them. It was fucked up. The LAPD took away Freddy Kruger last month for beating up a guy right in front of his kids.

There was talk from the cops about shutting their whole thing down. Making it illegal to dress up in costumes and get tips.

"Panhandling," as the officer had said.

Batman hung out with Superman & Wonder Woman while doing his thing. The night before Wonder Woman and him had been drinking, smoking, and they fucked once—just before she told him what was on her mind.

"We got two new guys starting tomorrow."

"What?"

"Yeah. They came up to me on the street today, wanted to know if they could hang with us."

"Wha? What? Well . . . do they have costumes?"

"Yeah," she said, wrapped in the sheet on the bed and exhaling smoke. "These guys got a Green Lantern and a Robin costume. Really good quality, they showed me pictures. Hey, you'll finally have a Robin now! Isn't that great?"

"Shit . . . I don't know Diana . . . I was kinda liking our little threesome."

"Oh come on, Bruce. It'll be good," she said, wrapping her arms around him as he sat on the edge of the bed, looking out the window.

"We can finally get the big, group tips. Like what the H-Men got going."

"Alright. That's fine."

And the next day, there they were, Green Lantern & Robin. Wonderful costumes, like she said. Their hair color and overall appearance spot on.

"Hey there!"

"Hello Robin, Green Lantern."

Their gloved hands shook as they got acquainted. He couldn't help but like them. Nice guys, musicians, Rockabilly guys from Venice. They went out into the crowd of people, Superman's voice booming over the crowd telling everyone that they're safe from evil and wrong doers, *blah, blah, blah,* the usual bullshit that Superman always said.

Batman yelled to Robin over the enclosing crowd. They were now fully entrenched by people, fat & sweaty. But Batman's panic attack took over.

"COME ON!" Batman shouted over the rising crowd noise. The dynamic duo shoved & pushed parting the sea of fat tourists and breaking out onto the sidewalk.

"What's up, Batman?" Robin asked looking up to him for direction.

The size difference was just like in the comics. Robin was a little guy.

"We just need to get outta there. Let's go take a lap down Hollywood Boulevard . . . see what kinda cash we can grab."

"Okay, Batman."

They walked up and down the walk of fame posing for a few pictures, making some kids' day with wide-eyed excitement that would be with them forever. They made forty bucks too.

"Alright, that's good for now. Let's grab a beer, Robin."

It was a small dive on Hollywood Boulevard. They were two beers in and there was some real talk from Batman to Robin about how Hollywood really was. Robin was learning a lot.

"Yup. I moved out here in 1997. I saw that movie *Swingers* and I thought . . . I could do that, that could be my life, I want that."

"And what happened, Bats?"

"Well . . . I came out here, went to film school, did everything I was told, and . . . I still got fucked," he said, taking a long pull from the bottle.

"Well what happened exactly?"

"Well . . . ya see . . . when I was in film school, the instructors all told us . . . you either do your internship here in Hollywood or go to New York. Anywhere else and you won't be able to make it. That's what they said."

"Yeah?"

"Yeah. So I did my internship here in Hollywood and it was for nothing. The whole two years that I was at Paramount, I was never allowed to even touch any film equipment. Well, just to dust it off and clean it. But they didn't even try to teach me anything there. I got them their Starbucks in the morning, did food runs at lunch, and took out the trash. I swept the parking lot, cleaned the toilets, I was a fucking janitor at that place. And you know what happened next?"

"Huh?"

"One day they just fired me. Just like that. After two years of being their bitch boy. So now I have $50,000 in student loans that I can't pay back, and a degree that got me nowhere."

"Fuck," Robin said, finishing his beer.

"Yeah. So . . . what do you do?"

"I'm in school for audio engineering."

"Ah . . . the music business, eh?"

"Yeah, Batman."

"Hmm."

Batman grew silent then, just finishing his beer and staring into the mirrored wall.

He *wanted* to say:

I have 117 scripts sitting in a stack next to my TV. That's eight screenplays a year. Robin, I've been at this for fourteen years and it doesn't get any better. I never stop trying and I keep at it, year after year. But I'm done. Get out while you still can, Robin. This city will eat you, rape you, kill you. If you still have a home, I suggest you go back to it."

Batman sat, his beer finished, and continued to stare straight ahead in thought. Robin pulled out a ten-dollar bill, smiling, calling for the bartender. He had that sparkle in his eye of youth and hope.

Batman didn't want to say all that shit, crush that gleam in Robin's eye—the same gleam he once owned.

Those were the best days—

the great days

the glory days

to be young, handsome, poor, and hopeful

and believe you could make it,

that it could happen.

So Batman didn't say another word about it.

Nope.

There were things Robin would have to learn all on his own.

K.J. Hood, the Pro Wrestler

K.J. Hood, the pro wrestler, had paralyzed a guy in the ring. It was an accident, a miscommunication about what move to do next. It took him eight years to make it to the big time, the WWF. The guy he hurt ended up paralyzed from the neck down, so it wasn't long before the WWF gave him the pink slip.

Living with his mother, he was now back on the independent circuit, wrestling on weekends for 100 bucks a night (one of the higher paid wrestlers on the indy circuit) at fairgrounds and in bingo halls, getting pinned by guys younger than him—future titleholders and superstars. He wasn't young anymore. His knees were bad—he needed replacements in both, or at least painkillers to help him through. But with no health insurance and no real work history besides wrestling he was fucked.

His cousin Rick told him about a guy who sold everything. Anything a guy would need—he had it. But this dude was in a real bad neighborhood, warning K.J. not to go there after dark. You may not know it, but in certain areas, Little Rock, Arkansas is a pretty dangerous place, where the Bloods & Crips control the streets and the pigs know to stay out.

Thinking nothing of it, K.J. threw on some navy blue track pants, his blue Chuck Taylor's and a white wife beater. His still hulking, black torso swelled up as he stood in front of the mirror one last time.

He parked his little black car, got out and began walking the vast concrete apartment complex, searching for # 213. He went to all three levels but couldn't find it. K.J. walked back out onto the street, cell phone in hand, calling his cousin when a red car pulled up, "Jam On It" bumping from the stereo so loud it rattled the windows and shook the concrete sidewalks.

The passenger window rolled down, "HEY! . . . FOO!" K.J. turned to the skinny-faced kid in the passenger seat, his hands in his lap, covered by a red bandana. "Yeah, YOU, nigga! Where da fuck you from?!"

This is it, he thought. This young kid was about to pull up a sawed-off shotgun and this is how it would end for him. No more looking for jobs, no more bills, no more disappointment, no more guilt, no more pain. Those knees wouldn't matter anymore.

Nothing would.

And he was fine with it.

But that didn't mean he was going out like a punk bitch. He still had his pride.

"I said, where you from, bitch?"

K.J. stared at him hard and his voice boomed, "The WWF mothafucka!" He raised his arms up stuck his chest out and flexed hard everything he had.

The silence seemed to last an eternity before the skinny kid shouted, "AHH SHIT! This be muhfuckin' K.J. nigga!"

"What?!" voices from inside shouted. The back windows rolled down.

"Oh! Shiiiit! What up K.J.? That match with The Undertaker was classic, homie!"

"Yeah dawg, you a favorite down south! What you doin' down here?"

K.J. relaxed his tense shoulder muscles and smiled big, laughing and wiping away sweat.

Turned out the dealer he was looking for was the skinny kid in the front seat.

He gave the pills to him, half-off that first night.

K.J.'s still wrestling, still living at his mom's house and buying pills from those Bloods every week. They often laugh about the night they met K.J., and how he almost got his ass shot.

Crash Kills Boy Rockstar:
The Dark and Lonely Street of Eddie Cochran

Oh Eddie Cochran. What were you thinking that night as the taxi began to spin out of control and your girlfriend screamed?

Were you thinking about Buddy? Did you know that this was the end? I know you did.

After Buddy, Ritchie, and The Bopper were all killed, you said you should've been on that plane, too, and that you were next.

Afterall, it was you, Eddie, who talked Holly into doing that tour. He sat in his New York apartment with his pregnant wife on the phone with you, reluctant to go. But when you said, "Oh come on, Holly. I'd go if you asked me," he couldn't say no.

Then at the last minute your agent pulled you off the tour to do *The Ed Sullivan Show* and your life was spared.

When you heard about the crash, you knew *you* should've been on that plane too. You were living on borrowed time, and you knew it.

You spent your last nights drinking whiskey until you blacked out, after pounding on the chest of a hotel manager, shouting, screaming, wailing, "My God, I'm gonna die and no one can stop it!"

That night they had to call a doctor to the hotel in Manchester to sedate you. And it was the strangest thing when you awoke the next day, you were different. Your fear was gone. There was a calmness about you, Eddie. You told your road manager to go out and buy every Buddy Holly record he could find. Which was odd, because after his death you couldn't bear to hear his music. A song of Buddy's would come on the radio and you would quickly turn the station. But now, you told your girlfriend that "It's gonna be okay. I'm gonna see Buddy again, soon."

You knew.

Before the taxi hit that concrete lamp post, when it started to spin, you covered your girlfriend with your own body. When thrown out the car door, your head scraped the roof of the car, which had busted open and the metal sliced into your head, and across your skull and into your brain. Then you skidded two hundred feet on the back of your skull.

Were you scared Eddie?

Could you see Buddy, Ritchie, and The Bopper putting out a cigarette under the yellow streetlight, waiting to take you to the other side? Leaving behind the screaming girls, tailored suits, unmatched guitar solos, smoking reefer in the desert, shooting your guns, the scent of American virgins, and a good smoke after a meal.

An elderly couple found you in the street, blood coming out your ears, nose, and mouth. Deep lacerations crossed your skull, staining your blonde hair red with blood.

The taxi had been used for a wedding earlier that day and confetti covered the inside of the white Ford Consul and now it was all over the road, some still blowing around in the air, scattered along the street with your clothes, your guitar, Buddy Holly records, and autographed 8x10s of your face signed,

Don't Forget Me,
    Eddie Cochran.

Danny Valdez was born in the low-end suburb of Mesa, Arizona. What is so astonishing about Danny is not that he triumphed over an unconventional childhood filled with guns, alcohol, and some neglect, but rather how he embraces and cherishes his complicated boyhood, with all its flaws. His story is heartbreaking, comical, and insightful—an openhearted and audaciously honest portrayal of a mixed Mexican/white boy emerging into adulthood.

BOOKS BY SUN DOG PRESS

Steve Richmond, *Santa Monica Poems*

Steve Richmond, *Hitler Painted Roses*
(Foreword by Charles Bukowski and afterword by Mike Daily)

Steve Richmond, *Spinning Off Bukowski*

Neeli Cherkovski, *Elegy for Bob Kaufman*

Randall Garrison, *Lust in America*

Billy Childish, *Notebooks of a Naked Youth*

Dan Fante, *Chump Change*

Robert Steven Rhine, *My Brain Escapes Me*

Fernanda Pivano, *Charles Bukowski: Laughing With the Gods*

Howard Bone with Daniel Waldron, *Side Show: My Life with Geeks,
Freaks & Vagabonds in the Carny Trade*

Jean-François Duval, *Bukowski and the Beats*

Dan Fante, *A gin-pissing-raw-meat-dual-carburetor-
V8-son-of-a-bitch from Los Angeles*

David Calonne, Editor, *Charles Bukowski, Sunlight Here I Am:
Interviews and Encounters, 1963-1993*

Ben Pleasants, *Visceral Bukowski, Inside the Sniper
Landscape of L.A. Writers*

Chandler Brossard, *Over the Rainbow? Hardly*
(Introduced and edited by Steven Moore)

Dan Fante, *Short Dog*

Dan Fante, *Kissed By A Fat Waitress*

Pam "Cupcakes" Wood, *Charles Bukowski's Scarlet*